Nine Lives

Are you ready?

Author J. D. Ellison

Copyright © 2025 by J. D. Ellison

All rights reserved. No part of this book may be reproduced in any form without written permission from the publisher, except in the case of brief quotations embodied in critical articles or reviews.

This is a work of fiction. Names, characters, places, and incidents are the product of the author's imagination or are used fictitiously.

ISBN: 9798280615724

Printed in the United States of America

To my remarkable wife, my muse and amazing editor. Thank you for always loving and supporting me, especially on this book. I could not have done this without you. I look forward to working together on the sequel and seeing where this journey takes us. I love you most sweetheart.

Nine Lives
Author J. D. Ellison

Table of Contents

Chapter 1 *Cian: About Me* 7

Chapter 2 *Cian: War* 26

Chapter 3 *Clare: The Curse* 38

Chapter 4 *Cian: The Group* 59

Chapter 5 *Inara: Apology Accepted... Eventually* 87

Chapter 6 *Abacus: Unraveling* 106

Chapter 7 *Cian: The Date* 119

Chapter 8 *Jameson: Not Ready* 145

Chapter 9 *Inara: Fate* 157

Chapter 10 *Cian: Impatience* 177

Chapter 11 *Cian: Under Pressure* 191

Chapter 12 *Inara: Scorned* 205

Chapter 13 *Cian: The Storm* 218

Chapter 14 *Cian: Unhinged* 239

Chapter 15 *Abacus: No way out* 251

Chapter 16 *Cian: The Darkness* 258

Chapter 17 *Cian: Help Wanted* 274

Chapter 18 *Cian: Last Stand* 285

NINE LIVES

CHAPTER 1
CIAN: ABOUT ME

My name is Cian Rowe, and my story begins in the vibrant city of Chicago where the scent of metal floats in the wind and you can easily disappear in the shadows of the skyscrapers and bustle of the city. I lived a dark and tragic life, burdened with a power few could ever imagine. My childhood was a mix of pure joy and profound sorrow—a time of innocence punctuated by the harsh realities of life and death. It was a delicate dance between light and shadow, shaping the course of my existence forever.

I always thought that I was an ordinary kid with an overactive imagination and practically limitless freedom, as my parents were not ones to worry about my safety. Some of my friends thought they seemed odd and distant, but I was grateful for the chance to explore without a chaperone. I took their lack of concern as a sign that they trusted me and were simply working hard at the store to provide a stable home. Back then, my biggest worries were running out of quarters at the arcade and not beating the high score in Galaga.

That all came to a crashing halt the day I learned the harsh truth about death. It was the first domino to fall, setting off a cascade of events that would change my life forever—though you're not ready for that part yet. I do long for the days of blissful ignorance that I once took for granted. The holidays were my favorite time of year, especially when we visited my Aunt Clare's house. I'll always remember the year we scrambled to prepare for Y2K, convinced the world would end at midnight. I probably should have been scared, but the idea of no more school or homework completely overshadowed the whole "end of the world" scenario my parents kept warning about.

I had no real understanding of the gravity of such events or their consequences. Aunt Clare, however, remained calm, as if she knew nothing would happen—or perhaps because she had more important things to worry about than a phony doomsday. Aunt Clare had been a widow since I was six. I was too young to really understand what had happened to Uncle Jay. Everyone just said it was sudden and tragic. I don't remember much about him, but Aunt Clare always told me I reminded her of him, which made me feel connected to him in a small but comforting way.

She would say I had his kind heart and, on occasion, would comment that my eyes were the same as his. She always said we both loved her more than she deserved. I do have one memory of him taking me to the Lincoln Park Zoo, which is probably why it's my favorite zoo in the world. Uncle Jay had volunteered to take me to school that day, but instead, to my surprise, he took me to the zoo for the best day ever. He told me it was our day to do whatever we wanted, and we could stay until we had seen every animal. He knew so much about each one and taught me about the snow leopard—how they can't actually roar like other big cats but have an ear-splitting yowl. That experience stayed with me all these years, and I still treasure that day of freedom with him.

Sometimes, it felt like I stayed with Aunt Clare more than my own parents, but I loved it. She had never been able to have kids of her own and helped raise me while my parents ran the store and did whatever parents do. Now that I think of it, I don't actually know what they did most of the time. I know they worked hard to provide for us, but I never really understood what they sold in that old store. I remember my dad saying they had whatever people needed—for a price. They worked odd hours, and I recall many late nights and weekends that pulled them away.

The store was downtown, but we lived in the north suburbs, so they would drop me off at Aunt Clare's on the way since she lived in Lincoln Park, not far from Wrigley Field. I loved spending my weekends at Cubs games with her and sneaking off to explore the massive city together whenever we wanted. It was more exciting than Saturday morning cartoons to me. We would take the L to Wrigley for games, and though the sheer number of people packed in like sardines sometimes made me nervous, the thrill of the adventure always outweighed the discomfort.

One night when we were coming home late from a game some guy pulled a knife on us and demanded cash or he would gut us. Aunt Clare stared him down and did not blink, as if he wasn't even a threat. One second the stranger had a knife and stepped toward us and the next thing I know he is on the ground and Aunt Clare is pulling my arm to get off the train. I was only seven that time and still ignorant to Death.

As scary as that was, she was my best friend, and I always knew I was safe with her. I loved my aunt dearly and idolized her in every way, she was the coolest person and lived the life I wanted to when I grew up. She had an amazing house with a huge backyard, a pantry always stocked with our favorite gummy bears, and the best dog ever, Shelby. All of my memories of back then are happy with only one that stands out as not. Aunt Clare got mad when I told her my birthday wish was to have blue eyes just like hers. I wanted to match her glacial blue eyes that I could have sworn glowed in the dark too. Before I knew what was happening there was yelling.

"Never wish for that! I would gladly be rid of them if I could."

Typically, Aunt Clare was calm and patient, so it was shocking to see her so rattled by my wish, but we never spoke of it again and ten minutes later were eating cake and laughing like it never happened in the kitchen. My childhood was happy and normal until a single moment changed my life forever. You never forget the day you die, for the first time. Mine started like so many ordinary days do by being dropped off to stay with my aunt for the weekend. I ran into the house to greet my best friend, Shelby. She was a beautiful lab mix that Aunt Clare adopted from a local shelter; she said that we were both born on the same day and that it was fate that Aunt Clare picked her. Aunt Clare made a point to get Shelby and I matching gifts every year to celebrate. For our ninth birthday she got us matching Cubs jerseys. I got Wood and Shelby got Sosa. But I am getting off track again.

I was, a boring nine-year-old, chasing his favorite pup outside on a crisp sunny fall day. It was just after Halloween, so the trees were beginning to lose their vibrant shades of yellow, orange, and red with leaves littered on the ground. I loved making piles and jumping into them feeling them crunch under my weight, Shelby did too. She was barking at a squirrel and chasing it along the fence line as it jumped from tree to tree taunting her. Those large oaks in the back gave the squirrels great escape routes to mess with Shelby.

Suddenly a cold chill crawled up my spine and the air went stale, leaving me with a strange sense of dread. I no longer heard Shelby barking and the squirrel was oddly floating in midair, as it was jumping to a new branch before Shelby could get it. Shelby was frozen in place not moving a muscle, which creeped me out. I ran inside to get help.

"Aunt Clare, come quick! Something is wrong with Shelby!" I shout as I enter the house.

I see a strange man standing across from Aunt Clare in the kitchen, he looks puzzled as I run to her, pulling on her hand and unable to look away from the stranger until she pulled my chin toward her. In all my years with Aunt Clare she never invited anyone over, except my parents and me of course. She has a look of terror on her face, and it transfers to me when I see a tear fall and roll down her cheek. I refuse to let it control me but am very aware of the fear building inside.

"Aunt Clare, who is that? Are you ok?"

I have no idea what I just got in the middle of and what consequences will follow. She kneels down to meet me eye level as her tears run down her face. It is hard to take my eyes off the stranger and especially the gold ring he is carrying. I have never seen anything like it. It is about the size of my soccer ball and has one row of beads on it, which remind me of the abacus counter on my aunt's desk that I love to play with when she works on her grants and stuff. The gold ring is mesmerizing in a way that intrigues me, but I am not sure why.

"Cian, love, I need you to go upstairs and call your parents from the phone in my room. Wait there until they come for you," she says sternly, but there's a sadness in her voice that settles deep in my core, stirring something loose.

"No! I am not leaving!" I demand, my voice cracking.

I can't leave her with this stranger, not while she is crying and probably afraid. It's the first time I've ever seen her show what she would call weakness. She is always tough and tells me I need to stop leaking every time I cry. She always says to take a minute to fix it, then we'd talk through my emotions so I wouldn't let them rule me. But I know something is wrong, and this stranger is a problem. She's afraid of him, I can see it. Did he break in to rob us? My mind leaps back to our movie night. Star Wars is one of our favorites, and Aunt Clare always says Darth Vader reminds her of someone she knew—someone powerful like him. Could this be her Darth Vader? My little brain is trying its best to piece things together, but I'm out of my depth, and out of time.

"Are you ready?" The stranger asks, his deep, ominous tone sending a chill up my spine.

It's the scariest thing I've ever heard. I thought the snow leopards' yowls were ear-splitting, but this guy? This guy is deadly. Aunt Clare always stresses the importance of controlling my emotions no matter what, but I can't sit back and let this stranger hurt her.

"Are you ready?" the stranger repeats, his voice sharper this time.

A strange energy pulses through me, something foreign yet familiar, and before I know it, I yell:

"No! I won't let you hurt her. Leave us alone!"

I hug my aunt as tightly as I can, my heart hammering in my chest, as the golden ring in the stranger's hands explodes with green light. A second row of beads appears from nowhere, one glowing green before vanishing. I freeze in shock, then squeeze my eyes shut, holding onto Aunt Clare, willing this to be a nightmare I'll wake up from any second.

Aunt Clare clutches me with so much strength I can barely breathe. When I finally open my eyes, the stranger is gone. I don't know what just happened, but Aunt Clare and I are safe. I can hear Shelby barking again, and for a moment, all seems right with the world. But Aunt Clare doesn't let go. She holds onto me like she's afraid I'll disappear if she does.

That night was both the best and worst of my life. I saved my aunt—but I also made an enemy of Fate. When Aunt Clare finally releases me, she smiles, but her eyes remain sad.

"Your father would be so proud of you."

She pauses, then corrects herself.

"I mean, I am proud of you. And don't worry, Death is gone," she says, patting my head.

"Who was that, Aunt Clare?" I ask, my voice barely above a whisper.

"You walked in on my Loss, Cian, and then you did the impossible—you saved me. You gave one of your nine lives to Abacus to save mine. You have so much to learn. You only have eight lives now… and you just woke up something I had hoped would stay dormant."

From that moment on, my life was never the same. I couldn't explain it at the time, but I felt a fundamental shift inside me, something that changed my life forever. I had used my first life to save my aunt, disrupting the natural order.

Aunt Clare used to tell me stories to help me understand. The first and most memorable was about Abacus. She told me that Abacus plays a vital role in maintaining order in the universe, keeping track of all living beings and their inevitable deaths.

"Everyone is born with exactly nine lives," she explained. "Each time you die, one resets you. But once all nine are gone, there are no more chances."

She went on to tell me that a select few have the ability to channel this power—to change Fate itself.

"You are one of them."

"These abilities allow us to alter our destiny, but doing so upsets the balance and can cause cataclysmic events. I need you to promise me you will never use your power again," Aunt Clare says, gripping my shoulders so I have no choice but to look into her piercing blue eyes.

"Okay. I promise, Aunt Clare," I say, not fully understanding how serious this request is, or how impossible it will be to keep.

"You need to be on guard at all times now, especially when you get emotional. Anger is dangerous. It can make you use your abilities without meaning to. Please remember—these abilities come with a cost, one almost always higher than you want to pay."

I didn't realize it then, but Aunt Clare was speaking from experience.

"These abilities are a curse, Cian," she says softly.

"And being an enemy of Fate… is a daunting existence. You must fight the desire to use them, especially to be a hero, like you did for me."

She pulls me into another hug, breaking her own record for most hugs in a single weekend. Aunt Clare was never someone you'd call affectionate. She was practical, always saying emotions just get you into trouble. But at that moment, she didn't let go. And neither did I.

"I won't use my powers, Aunt Clare. Honestly, I don't even know how I did it the first time," I say with an innocent smile.

She studies me for a moment, her expression unreadable, before finally nodding.

Later, she makes me promise to keep it all a secret.

"No one else would believe it, Cian. And it's dangerous for normal people to know the truth about death," she warns.

I agree without question. At the time, it feels like a small thing. I don't fully grasp the weight of what I'm swearing to keep hidden.

…

One year later, I break my promise. Sitting across from my father, I proudly recount the time I stopped Abacus from hurting Aunt Clare, hoping it will prove that I'm plenty old enough to go to my friend's lake house for the weekend. If I was brave enough to face Death, surely, I could handle a couple of nights away.

My father doesn't react the way I expect.

Instead of being impressed, he simply says, "You're not old enough to go away for the whole weekend. We haven't even met his parents."

At ten years old, I think his reasoning is ridiculous. I was old enough. I had already saved a life! But in hindsight, I see his point. And worse, I see my mistake. I never should have told him. I was too young, too reckless, too blind to realize how right Aunt Clare had been about keeping it all a secret. I thought I was winning him over, proving something. Instead, I gave my parents the excuse they had been waiting for. They never liked how close I was with Aunt Clare. They always thought she was strange, that she had too much influence over me. And now, they pounced on the opportunity.

That night, they called her unstable. Unsafe. That night, they took her away from me. I never saw her again. They told me Aunt Clare wasn't well and that she needs medical help. My reaction to the news was extreme. I ran away and tried to make it to Aunt Clare's house on foot. My parents caught me before I was even a mile from the house and brought me back. I subsequently refused to speak to either of them for the next year. Which led to years of therapy talking to shrinks who only wanted to convince me that it was all made up and that Clare was a sick woman who needed help. The saddest thing is that I eventually lost sight of the truth and grew numb to everything and everyone.

Aunt Clare died the night I betrayed her and told our secret. I was not there to save her from Abacus this time. I didn't get to say goodbye or to apologize for failing her. I was not there for her when she needed me and she died knowing I betrayed her. Shelby died that night too. In an instant, I lost my best friends and it was all my fault. I overheard my dad say something about it that night to my mom when they thought I was asleep, but it didn't make any sense so I disregarded it as a misunderstanding. I was emotional and tired; there was no way I was hearing them right. They couldn't be talking about Abacus.

...

The years that followed were lonely. I drifted away from everyone, afraid that I'd let them down and lose them just like I lost Aunt Clare. Just like I lost Shelby. My parents buried themselves in work, leaving me alone more often than not. Instead of spending weekends at my aunt's house, I spent them in silence.

Three new schools. Too much therapy. And then, finally, I was "cured."

On my sixteenth birthday, I told my therapist what they wanted to hear, that I made it all up. The powers, the Loss, Abacus. Just a scared kid spinning stories. That's all. They signed off on my progress and set me free. I convinced myself I was moving on.

I had friends again, like Mike. I was making plans, living a normal life. And for the first time, it felt real. That's why, when my parents finally caved and let me borrow the Mustang to drive to a concert downtown, I felt something I hadn't in years. Hope. Maybe I really was going to be okay. Maybe I wasn't just faking it. Most of the time, I pretended to be the person I thought people wanted me to be and prayed they wouldn't see through me. You'd be surprised only one person ever did. I was driving too fast. The Mustang wasn't a car tonight; it was the Millennium Falcon. The speed, the rush, the thrill of finally having some control over my life.

Then—

"POP!"

A sound like a gunshot. The wheel jerked. My heart stopped. I fought to steer back onto the road, but the car had a mind of its own. The median came too fast, 88 miles per hour too fast. Impact. Silence. Everything froze. The music cut out. The world stood still. I know this feeling.

Déjà vu crept up my spine, chilling me to my core. The air felt wrong—stale, empty. Birds hovered motionless in the sky.

And then, her. A woman. Standing just outside the car, watching me. I moved as if through water, stepping out of the wreckage, my heartbeat hammering in my ears. I knew what this was. I think I just died and now I am in the limbo between living and dead.

"Do you know what's going on?" I ask, even though I already know the answer.

The woman doesn't blink. Doesn't move. Her expression is empty, hollow. Then she says.

"Are you ready?"

The words hit me like a punch to the gut. That same question. That same cold, inescapable voice. The stranger from my childhood. The one who had come for Aunt Clare.

Abacus! My eyes dart to the golden ring in her hands. This time, it only had one row of eight beads. I swallow hard. My mouth is dry.

"Where is my Aunt Clare?"

Abacus's gaze is fathomless, cutting straight through me, revealing nothing. I have no idea if she even recognizes me—if it is Abacus or just one of many.

"Are you ready?"

The words ring in my head, vibrating through my skull until I fall to my knees, clutching my ears. I can't fight it. I can't stop myself from answering.

"No."

One bead shifts on the row, no glowing this time though. Abacus disappears. I am kneeling in the middle of the road alone. Everything is back to normal, almost. Engines roar. Headlights blur. Horns blaring as cars fly past me, oblivious to what had just happened. I barely have time to roll out of the way before a semi-truck thunders past, missing me by inches.

Then—

My car. I turn just in time to watch the Mustang hit a pothole, the same one that had triggered the events leading to the loss of yet another life and put me back into Abacus's orbit. My tire blows, sending the car careening into the median. It flips. Crashes. Lands upside down. I should be in there.

But I'm not.

Abacus hadn't reset me properly, just like at Aunt Clare's. I should have been able to fix this. For a long, breathless moment, I wait for the explosion that never comes. Then, reality hits. The cops will be here soon. My parents. I need a story. Something believable. I climb back into the wreck, squeezing into the driver's seat just enough to buckle myself in. My hands are shaking. It took longer than it should have, but finally—

Click.

I barely have time to close my eyes before the sirens arrive. Seven lives left. I should be more careful. Should be smarter. Should have listened to what Aunt Clare taught me instead of trying to pretend I was normal. But even now, I feel Abacus. Every single day. Watching. Waiting. I decide to do the only thing I can, I hide. I keep my shields up at all times. I push people away. No more friends. No more risks. I won't use my abilities. I won't let Abacus take me. And maybe—just maybe—if I had listened to Aunt Clare from the start, her end would have been different, too.

Keeping my shield up at all times drains me. It makes me irritable, practically an asshole. And really, who wants to be friends with someone who feels dead inside? An emotionless husk that is focused on avoiding the unavoidable at all times.

"Noone does." I whisper to my invisible friends.

Have you ever gone without food and water for so long that all you can think about is survival? That gnawing emptiness clawing at you, making it impossible to focus on anything else? That's what isolation felt like for me. Cut off from the world. Cut off from my own parents. I had to pour every ounce of energy into my shields, or else I'd risk facing him.

Risk facing Abacus. Every time a neighbor experienced a Loss—which happened more often than you'd think, I had to be ready. The first time I wasn't. I woke up in the middle of the night, gasping, only to realize time had stopped. A Loss had happened while I slept. I hid under my covers, willing it to pass, but I felt Abacus just outside my window. Watching. Waiting.

Most people answer quickly to keep Losses from dragging on, but once, at school, I didn't realize I had stepped too far. I took more than a dozen steps before the reset hit, only I didn't reset. To everyone else, I had just teleported. Temptation gnawed at me. If I could move during a Loss, what else could I do? Could I stay there in limbo longer? Could I change things? Maybe this could be a superpower I use to fight crime.

But Aunt Clare's warnings echoed in my head, stopping me before I did something I couldn't take back. The weight of knowing about Abacus is crushing. Teenage hormones and Calculus are bad enough, but I have to live with the constant fear of slipping, of seeing him again. I adapt.

I install anti-slip ducks in my shower. I pad every sharp edge in the house. My parents don't question it when I tell them it's for a school project. I watch them closely because they're both down to their last lives, and the temptation to save them is unbearable. So, I reduce as much risk as possible. I get really good at calculating threats, minimizing danger. And for a while, I trick myself into believing it's enough. But it isn't. Three months before my eighteenth birthday, my parents go out for their anniversary. A drunk driver runs a red light.

I wasn't there to save them. The loss swallows me whole. I feel myself fold inward, burying the pain under layers of numbness. It's the only way I can function. I don't process anything until a child services agent knocks on my door, asking about next of kin. That's when it hits me. I'm alone. Truly, completely alone. She gives me a few weeks to find family I already know doesn't exist. When she comes back, her patience is gone. She threatens foster care. She doesn't care about me. She just wants to close the file and move on. Fine. I can give her that.

"Look," I say, turning on every ounce of charm I can fake.

"I'm out of family, but I'll make you a deal. I'll enlist today if you sign the paperwork."

She hesitates. "What branch honey?"

The question catches me off guard. My brain scrambles for an answer and lands on the one that promises swords and dragons, at least based on a commercial I saw once.

"The Marines!"

She doesn't care what I choose. She just wants me off her list. The recruiter can't believe how fast I sign the papers. Before I know it, I'm on a bus to San Diego, leaving behind Abacus and everything I'm too afraid to face. I didn't think this through but I just know I need to do something.

Serving my country feels like the first good thing I can do with my life. Maybe I can be a hero. Maybe I can finally stop running. And hell, maybe—just maybe—I'll find a way to put a bullet in Abacus.

CHAPTER 2
CIAN: WAR

The Marine Corps taught me how to shoot, how to survive, how to be patient, and how to kill. When I first arrived at boot camp, I had this grand idea that I'd be like Rambo or John Wayne—unstoppable, larger than life. I figured we'd spend our time charging into battle, guns blazing. I should have went Air Force.

Reality hit fast. Ninety percent of the time, we trained. The other ten percent? Sitting around, pretending to be busy so the higher-ups wouldn't make us do something pointless—like inventory every single item in the supply room or searching for a can of A-I-R.

But deployment? That gave me more adventure than I ever bargained for. I was squad leader in Second Platoon, recently promoted to Sergeant. Less than four years in, and I was already climbing the ranks—an accomplishment that, of course, never went to my head. Cough.

"Sergeant Rowe, report!" Captain Bell barked.

"Yes, sir! Second Platoon is ready to go. Oorah!" I responded, giving my squad a once-over to make sure everyone was squared away for our first mission.

"Sergeant, fall out and report to Major Westgate. He has your orders. Don't fuck it up. Oorah."

"Yes, sir! Squad, wait for me by the vehicles. Dismissed!"

I made my way to the command tent, where only officers and intelligence personnel were allowed. The second I stepped inside; someone pulled me to a desk and shoved a notepad in my hand.

"This is a routine compliance check of a village five miles due east," Major Westgate said, his voice flat.

"Your squad is to observe and report. You are not cleared to engage!"

The Major had been in the Corps longer than most of us had been alive. A for-lifer—the type of Marine who didn't just serve, he believed in the mission. He was squared away, had seen his share of combat, and we followed his orders without question.

I nodded. "Understood, sir."

Back with my team, I laid it out for them.

"Alright, listen up. Our mission is a security sweep of a small village five miles east of base. Intel says it's been empty for three days. Should be routine, but I want everyone ready for contact. Keep your head on a swivel—complacency gets Marines killed."

As I spoke, the thud-thud-thud of incoming mortars cut through the air. Welcome to Taji, Iraq. We hit the deck as the base went into lockdown. Dust rained from above. A few seconds passed before the all-clear sounded, and we were back on mission.

I passed around maps with our route and aerial surveillance images, and we geared up. The roads were pure shit—bumpy, uneven, forcing us to crawl along at thirty miles per hour unless we wanted our trucks to shake apart. At this point, they were held together by duct tape and esprit de corps. The desert sun stalked us the whole way. Sweat dripped down my back. I missed air conditioning. Almost as much as I missed pizza and a damn good cup of coffee.

"Hey, Sergeant, what's the first thing you're going to do when we get back home?" Lance Corporal West asked.

"That's easy, West. Bang your mom."

The squad broke into laughter.

"Now get your head in the mission. We're two minutes out."

Months ago, we cut power and sealed off the town's only well, forcing out anyone who might've tried to stay. It was too close to base—too high of an elevation. Command wanted it empty, so we made sure it stayed empty. Regular patrols, constant sweeps. This was just another one.

"Listen up, Devil Dogs!" I called out as we neared the village. "Command did not clear us to engage. We're here to observe and report. If we find anyone still here, they're presumed hostile—treat them as such. Stick to your zones, watch your six. Move out!"

I stopped the convoy a quarter mile out and ordered everyone to offload. Two Marines stayed behind to guard the vehicles and serve as our extraction if things got hot. I didn't expect resistance. But I always planned for worst-case scenarios. We approached a dilapidated barn on the west side of the village. The first shot rang out before we even crossed the threshold.

"Contact! Take cover!" I shouted.

Bullets tore through the rotting wood as we scrambled for cover. I raised my rifle and fired in the direction of the shooter, suppressing fire just long enough for my squad to get into position.

"What are you waiting for, Marines? Return fire!"

"Sergeant, we're not cleared to engage without command approval!"

I grit my teeth. "You want to walk home? You better start engaging that threat! Aim at that house and lay down fire!"

"Lance Corporal West, exit the barn and flank the shooter! We'll cover you!"

West hesitated for half a second before nodding.

"Private First-Class Jackson, Lance Corporal Cruz—controlled bursts at the threat! Go, West!"

West was barely nineteen. Most of my squad was young—too young for this war. Too young to drink but old enough to die. I wasn't much older, but I felt ancient in comparison. These guys weren't just my team. They were my family. The family I found after losing the one I was born with. And I wasn't about to let anything happen to them. An explosion erupts outside the barn. The force of it rattles my ribs. My gut twists. Grenade!

"Help! Sergeant." West's voice cut through the dust and gunfire.

I don't hesitate.

"Hold your positions!" I order. "I'm going after him."

Then I run. A single high-velocity round hums past me, followed by a second that finds the wounded Lance Corporal just as our eyes meet. I can't stop. I can't falter. My squad still needs me to get them out of this mess.

I take a deep breath, and the air shifts—stale, cold, replacing the blistering heat. I don't drop my shield, but I hesitate. The urge to save West is strong. A shot nearly takes out my knee, snapping me back to reality. I dive behind a rusted vehicle, heart pounding.

The moment passes, and I know West is gone. Abacus took him, and I did nothing. Like a coward. What's the point of having this ability if I don't use it to save the people who deserve it? The people I care about?

"Team, on my position now! We need to eliminate that shooter."

My squad moves fast, taking cover just outside the barn with me. West's body lies only a few feet away, still bleeding into the red dirt. They don't know what I do—West is already gone. Sunlight flashes off a muzzle as the hostile opens fire again.

"I got him! Second story, left window." I knife-hand toward the target.

We need to stop the shooter, but they have explosives. We have to keep our distance. I won't lose anyone else because of my orders.

"Stay down and wait for my signal," I yell, sprinting toward the backside of a structure that should give me a clear line of sight.

I push my body to its limit, sliding onto my knee as I reach the end of my cover. I steady my sights, waiting for him to peek out.

Slow, steady breath. I pull the trigger.

"One down," I sound off, letting my squad know I got him.

An impact an inch above my Kevlar makes me drop, crawling to cover. I spot the shooter—less than 200 yards out. An easy shot for a Marine and his rifle.

"Steady. One shot, one kill," I whisper, centering my aim, controlling my breath. I squeeze the trigger.

My round cuts through the air, a brief muzzle flash marking the moment before it finds its target. The hostile drops instantly. A chill crawls down my spine. Abacus is here again.

"Fuck yeah!" Jackson yells, stepping up from cover.

"Get down!" I barely get the words out before rounds start pinging off the vehicle next to him.

"Another shooter—take cover!" I bolt back to my team.

The third shooter is in the upstairs window of a neighboring house, only the muzzle flash visible as he sprays rounds at us. Sloppy. Untrained. He'll need to reload soon. I can't process West's loss—not yet. His body is still warm, eyes still staring at me as I reach my squad. My mind tries to drag me to that place, but I force it back. My shield slips, emotions pressing in, years of locked-away grief clawing for release.

"Sergeant, what do we do?" The Private's voice shakes.

Mission accomplishment comes first—that's drilled into us from day one. Semper Fidelis. Always faithful. It's tattooed across Lance Corporal West's back in huge block letters. I flash to the memory of giving him shit for getting it after watching Doom with the Rock. He thought he was invincible after that ink. I shove the thought aside.

"Jackson, Cruz—on me! We'll cover you. Move!"

"You got this, Sergeant," I remind myself. No time to check out.

We maneuver to the back of the property, prepping to breach the rear entrance. The shooter can't see us without exposing himself. That's all the time we need.

"Cruz, breach!"

Cruz kicks in the door—no problem for a guy built like a damn tank. More muscle than brains, but a good Marine. Wrote letters home to his six siblings every chance he got. A chill slams into me. Déjà vu. The door is rigged.

"Abacus."

The IED (improvised explosive devise) triggers the second Cruz's boot connects. The blast radius engulfs Cruz, Jackson, and me. They don't understand what's happening. They're frozen. Stuck in this limbo while I move freely. I scan for the reaper. I know why he's here. I won't let him take anyone else.

I spot the shooter's muzzle still in the window before turning back to Cruz and Jackson. Abacus stands in front of Cruz. I lock eyes with the death dealer. A teenage boy with curly brown hair this time. If not for the golden abacus in his hands, I'd never recognize Abacus.

"Are you ready?" The boy asks.

It catches me off guard. My first mistake. Before I can say a word—

"Yes." Cruz answers so fast as if he had been waiting for it.

Cruz vanishes. Gone as if he was never here. Just Jackson and me now. And Abacus. And the shooter upstairs. Shock hits me like a gut punch. Cruz accepted. Just… let go. I never considered what happens when someone willingly goes with Abacus. Why would he?

I can't breathe. West. Cruz. My men. My fault. Doubt crushes me. I let go of my control, rage surging in its place. I close my eyes. Deep breath. Aunt Clare's voice. Trust your instincts. Calm floods over me. I know what must be done. I tighten my grip on my rifle, the plastic handle bending slightly under my fingers. I charge.

Abacus turns to Jackson. "Are you ready?"

I pull the trigger.

"No, we aren't ready! Take my beads, you son of a bitch!"

The moment I say it, I know what the consequences are. Two beads on the golden ring start to glow green—plucked from a row that only had seven. Then Abacus vanishes before my round can reach him. I was so close. If I hadn't answered so fast, maybe I could have stopped it. But I also know Jackson might have answered yes instead, and I'm at peace with my decision.

That pull—Abacus's pull—is too strong. It drags the answer out of you, even if you don't want to give it. And the closer I was to him, the longer I waited to answer, the heavier that weight became. It reminds me of tactical water rescue training—treading water for hours, taking turns drowning each other while the other poor bastard fights to keep you afloat. Abacus is efficient. Maybe that's why Cruz answered yes. At his core, he was just… too tired to go on. And Abacus knew.

Cruz and West were close. We'd been deployed for months. Everyone was running on empty, the weight of war pressing down, making death seem like the easier option. Maybe, for Cruz, it was the better option. Then Abacus is gone, and everything picks up where it left off. Cruz kicks in the door. The IED blows. But this time, I'm far enough back. The blast doesn't reach me. Jackson is knocked off his feet, taking shrapnel.

"Jackson, you alright?" I push down on the wounds, trying to stop the bleeding.

He's unconscious, but he's not dead. Not yet. I want to vomit. West and Cruz are gone. Jackson is wounded. And I still have a shooter upstairs. If I don't act now, we're both next. I drag Jackson behind cover and radio for the cavalry. This is as bad as I'm going to let it get. I pop green smoke to mark the hostile's position and wait for the convoy to roll in.

"Five left, Cian. At this rate, you're not making it to a hundred."

I laugh. No one hears me. I'm frustrated. I'm exhausted. My ears are ringing from the blast. But I'm still here.

"Light it up!"

The rest of the squad pulls up and unloads. The building is reduced to rubble, ensuring every hostile inside is neutralized. I barely have time to process the destruction before I shove my shields back up—tight, unbreakable. Abacus won't get another chance to collect from me today. We load up Jackson, West, and Cruz, clear the rest of the village, and finish the mission.

I key my radio. "Mission accomplished. Village is clear. Two casualties, one wounded. En route. Over and out."

The next day, I visit Jackson in the med bay. He doesn't remember Abacus. Or anything after Cruz kicked the door. I don't ask. Even if he did remember, he wouldn't tell me. A Marine who can't fight is worthless in the eyes of the Corps. If he started talking about some supernatural grim reaper, they'd send him home. No more reenlistment. No more career service. And Jackson wants to be a lifer—thirty years in, no looking back. Me? I'm ready to get out now.

My mind won't shut up. Why did Cruz say yes? If my bullet had hit Abacus, would it have done anything? What the hell do I do now? By the time I finally get back to my tent, I strip out of my gear and drop onto my rack like a deadweight. The metal cot isn't comfortable—never has been. But tonight, after everything, it's just as good as a cloud. I could lie here forever.

Four down. Five left to go. A month later, my tour ends. I ship back to Camp Pendleton to finish out my service contract and learn new ways to bottle up my pain and keep moving forward.

...

Less than a year after that, I'm honorably discharged. I move to Chicago. Rent a small apartment near the Magnificent Mile. Technically, I own a house. But I'm not ready to go back there. Not ready to face Aunt Clare's memory. The last time I went there, I lost focus—just for a second. That was all it took. The neighbor slipped on the ice, and I felt Abacus stir. I barely managed to play dumb, act frozen, let it pass. But every time I go back, I feel her disappointment in me.

I'm not sure what's worse—knowing she's watching me. Or knowing she isn't.

CHAPTER 3
CLARE: THE CURSE

I don't want to believe it. But he's cursed too. I prayed it would skip him, that Fate would show mercy for once. But Fate only ever laughs at me. He doesn't even realize what's happening. Doesn't understand what he's unleashed by giving up a life to save me. I have to find a way to protect him from the pain of my mistakes. But I know—deep down—there's no escaping Fate now.

These abilities have been the cruelest curse of my life, and now, I have to watch them devour Cian just as they did me. When he gave that life for me, he didn't know what it would cost him. Didn't know the weight it would place on his soul. And worse, he has no idea the kind of danger this power brings. Given enough time and opportunity, it corrupts all of us. I learned that lesson the hard way. This power is anything but pure. It rots you from within before you even realize it.

I will start his training now. I only hope it will be enough to keep the darkness at bay. But he's so young. And I fear he won't learn quickly enough to actually protect himself. I need more time with him. And though he saved me today, Abacus will return. I'll teach him everything I know—the lessons I had to learn through suffering. I'll share my research when he's ready. If I can spare him even a fraction of the pain I endured, then maybe… maybe my life won't have been the tragedy I've always feared it to be.

His brown eyes cut through me as he looks up, silent, searching, lost. I open my mouth, but no words come. What could I possibly say to comfort him? That his Fate is sealed? That his kind, gentle nature will be destroyed before he's even grown? No. I lie.

"It'll be okay," I whisper, pulling him into a tight hug.

At first, the only way to hold his attention is through stories—knights and wizards, dragons and monsters. He listens well, even enjoys them. But the stories are more than just tales. They're lessons—history disguised as fantasy. Because the truth is too dangerous. This power will make it impossible for him to live a normal life. It always ends in tragedy. Should I take him in? Keep him with me? The thought refuses to let me rest.

He has no idea how much this ability will isolate him. How every death near him will pull him into its wake. How Abacus will never leave him alone once he realizes Cian has the power to free him. I only hope he understands the real meaning behind my stories—to warn him.

"We all repeat the patterns of our ancestors," I tell him.

"We either die early as heroes… or live long enough to become villains."

He listens carefully, taking in every word. I pray I'm not overdoing it. I pray Cian will never lose himself as I did. The scars of this power still weigh heavy on me. And I will never be free of them. Our ability allows us to give one of our lives to another, to save them. But an even rarer, far more dangerous gift exists. Some of us can take a life. There was once someone—just for a moment—who was even more powerful than Abacus himself.

He sacrificed everything to save the ones he loved. To know power, to taste it—it's intoxicating. But to know of power and never possess it? That can drive you to madness. This power feeds on our emotions, making it nearly impossible to control. Most who have it burn out before high school—trying to save every soul they come across. I was never that kind of hero. My great-grandmother died at sixteen. Just three months after giving birth to my mother.

She had five younger brothers to protect—her mother ran away when she was nine. And she used her ability to save them, to keep them safe from Abacus. But she didn't stop there. She gave every life she had to them. Even traded lives between them to extend their time far beyond what Fate intended. That's the danger of this power. Those who act out of anger or fear when facing Abacus will take a life for themselves.

Those who act out of love? They're even more blind. And in my experience, there are no limits to how far they'll go to save the ones they love.

"Love is the most dangerous emotion of all."

I only hope Cian learns to guard against it. He has the potential to break this curse. To do the impossible. But his heart is too kind. Too open. Already longing for love. Love got us into this. And love will not get us out. I pour everything I have into teaching him. I use stories. He listens. He learns.

"There are Fates worse than death," I warn him. "If you fail to follow my rules, you may find yourself on Fate's bad side."

It's a heavy lesson for a child. But time is short. If I die tomorrow, I need to know he's ready.

"Many before us have used this power for personal gain, to prolong their lives. But giving in to that temptation always leads to destruction. Taking lives is dangerous. More addictive than drugs. It feels like lightning in your veins, and once you start—once you deny fate itself—you'll never stop."

I take a breath, steady myself.

"Using our power consumes the wielder's soul. And once your soul is gone, you can't just get a new one. Remember that, Cian. Only God can make souls. Let's keep it that way."

Cian looks up at me, his voice small.

"Aunt Clare… what if I want to save Shelby?"

My heart breaks.

"Animals are different," I tell him gently.

"You can no more save Shelby from death than you could save the chicken we ate for dinner."

I expect him to cry. To protest. But he only nods, bracing himself for the next lesson. I swallow the lump in my throat. I am proud of him.

"Using this power too much will strip you of the single most important part of you," I say.

"You'll become an empty husk—going through the motions of life, but never able to feel it."

Cian pauses. Then, after a moment—

"Auntie, can we get some ice cream after this story?"

I blink, then chuckle. He is still so innocent and pure. I can't believe he is related to me.

"Maybe," I say.

"Now listen closely."

I don't tell him everything. Not yet. I don't tell him that the first of us—the ancestor who received this power—was said to have been gifted by an angel. That some believe it was a reward for saving the world. I never believed that. I think this curse came from somewhere else. But what I do know, what I believe, is that every single one of us has either fallen to darkness... or gone mad. A handful lived ordinary lives. Only because they never used their power.

Never let themselves get close to anyone. I look at Cian. He has to be different. He has to be the one to break the cycle. I never wanted children because I never wanted to pass this curse to them. And now, Cian is as young as I was when I lost my first life. The life that set me on this path. A path of regret. A path of torment. I will do everything in my power to make sure he doesn't suffer the same fate.

"Alexander the Great was one of the greatest wielders of power in history, yet even he eventually fell to the darkness. He used his abilities to conquer most of the world and survived more than a hundred deaths. He might have succeeded in his plan to rule forever if it weren't for Abacus and the fact that we lose our abilities once our souls burn out. Alexander is actually the first to burn out his soul, and that's why we now understand the limits of our powers. There's a natural order that keeps the scales balanced," I say, watching Cian hang on every word.

"As we grow stronger, so does Abacus, and that's something we must consider when using our powers. No rational person would want Abacus to gain more power. I often wonder, though, if Abacus grows in power, would we grow stronger too? It's a crazy thought, because Abacus is bound to serve and cannot change its power without help from one of us."

"Abacus has the most important job of accounting for all life in the world and ensuring we die when Fate demands it. After someone runs out of lives, Abacus reaps them. From what I've found in my research, he's actually responsible for taking the soul to its final resting place as well. It seems strange that Abacus is both an accountant and a taxi driver, but I suppose it's an efficient way to deal with all of us. Since he exists outside of time, it's not like he can't reach us all eventually," I say, a chill passing quickly through me.

"No one can escape Abacus, but some have managed to evade him longer than Fate intended. There is an old story of a woman who lived four lifetimes before finally being taken in peace by Abacus. The price for living beyond your nine lives is steep, and she used those around her to pay it for her. Cian, promise me you'll never be like that?" I beg, hoping he'll stay the pure-hearted boy he is for as long as possible.

Cian's small fingers slip into mine as we walk into the kitchen for a snack.

"Aunt Clare," he whispers, "I won't ever steal a life. I promise."

His hand is warm, so very alive, and I squeeze it tightly.

"Good." I murmur.

I feel a pang of regret for so many of my past decisions and wonder if I should just leave and never come back.

"Aunt Clare, can you teach me more about what happened?" he asks and looks up at me with such eager eyes, and my mind settles quickly.

I must help him understand. Perhaps this is how I can finally atone for my past.

"Once upon a time, I begin, there was a young girl struggling just to survive each day. She had to fight for food, often going hungry and cold, sleeping in the fields. One day, the girl's fate changed when she discovered she had hidden power within her all along. She grew into a woman, and with her power, she eventually became a queen, conquering many kingdoms. But it was never enough. Her power came with a secret cost, one she couldn't pay with jewels, gold, or art."

"No amount of money could pay what this power demanded as tribute, and the queen learned the hard way that you can't outrun Fate. Some have found ways to delay it or even trade with another, but no one can escape her. The queen used her power for personal gain for so many years and lived far beyond her time, stealing lives from those around her."

"Auntie, is that why you made me promise not to steal a life?" he asks, quickly catching on, and I feel a flicker of hope.

"Exactly. Now, back to our queen. In the end, she lost someone she loved more than life itself and eventually welcomed death as her friend, and they walked together into the Void," I say to Cian, who is sitting on the floor with Shelby, listening intently.

I don't tell him that the cost of taking another's life marks not only your soul but also affects your appearance and personality. The changes are the punishment for taking what isn't rightfully ours, marked so that everyone who sees us knows the truth and is warned to stay away or they too will end up losing more than they bargained for. Taking lives is rare, but not going mad afterward is even rarer. Most lose their sanity after one life, though some manage to live with the madness. There's a dark pull that twists you inside out, slowly eating away everything that makes you human. Eventually, everything that ties you to this world, including your humanity, disappears. The trick is to find something or someone to ground you here, a tether to this realm. Once your soul is truly burnt out, there's no repairing it, and unless you know an archangel or get an I owe you from the almighty, you are out of luck and time.

I still see every life I've taken. There's a darkness inside of me where my soul used to be, itching to break free and devour the world. I swear, if it weren't for Cian, I'd burn it all down. I've lived too long and need to face Fate before this sweet boy loses any more lives for me. I can't even look in a mirror without seeing what I've taken.

...

I was young, angry with the world, and thought this was all a gift the first time it happened. I thought I'd hit the lottery and was chosen. Maybe I could be a hero—or at least change my life. How naïve I was. I learned the hard way that taking a life is much more than just moving a bead on the abacus. The hard part is stopping once you start. It's intoxicating, the rush of power, and it makes you feel invincible. The withdrawals and the emotional and mental toll afterward are brutal, and some days, I think the lucky ones are those who break.

I'll leave my journal for Cian. I've written my entire life down for him, but I'm not brave enough to give it to him while I'm alive. I couldn't bear to see how he would look at me after reading it. There are so many atrocities I committed out of greed, a lust for power. I never did fill the empty void inside of me, but Cian helped slow its decline these last several years.

I teach Cian how to hide his abilities and shield himself from Abacus and others like us. It should keep him out of trouble for a little while, at least. As he grows older, he'll need to train to ensure the shields stay strong enough to manage his powers. The shield works by blocking our abilities, and in his current state, it's fairly easy. But once puberty hits, his emotions won't be the only thing in overdrive.

Without shields, we practically see Abacus everywhere, and that always leads to using our abilities to save a life or take one, as the pull to use them is stronger than our will. I wish I had more time to teach him, especially how powerful he will become. In an instant, his power could betray him. If he takes pity on someone who is fated to die, or worse, if he loves them, his abilities almost work on autopilot. Even worse is when we perceive the person as a villain in our minds.

It makes us want to see them face justice, and we might help ourselves to their last remaining lives as some kind of "civil service." The curse is that our minds can save lives one moment or, just as easily, steal a dozen without a second thought.

"Cian, come here. I want to teach you something special."

"Okay, Aunt Clare, coming. Come on, Shelby!" Cian hollers for Shelby to follow him out of the kitchen.

"Come sit with me on the floor. I want you to take a deep breath in and hold it. Imagine you're underwater and can't let it out."

"Okay, Aunt Clare," Cian says, taking a deep breath in.

"Good. Now slowly let it out as you close your eyes and imagine a blanket being wrapped around you. I want you to focus on the blanket covering you, protecting you from everything. Describe it in your mind. What does it feel like? Is it soft? Does it have blue on it?" I say in a calm voice, wrapping a blanket around him to help him relax.

Our thoughts drive our abilities, but emotion is the true fuel that ignites them. Being able to harness raw emotion is the most dangerous way to control our powers. It's hard to direct, but it holds the most potential. Some people choose anger because it comes naturally to them, while others choose love. Cian will need to master his power with a clear mind, free of emotions. I need him to gain control of his hormones and emotions before they get him killed, or worse.

These meditation techniques will keep him calm and help him activate his shield so it becomes second nature. He must learn to protect himself every day without even thinking about it.

"You can do it, Cian," I say with a soft smile as I feel his shield project outward, blocking him from my senses.

"You did it!" I shout and sweep him into a hug to celebrate his first shield.

It's not the strongest shield, but with practice, he'll be able to hide from Abacus. The key to shielding is visualizing the power flowing around you, not through you. The trickiest part is being able to tap into your power without Abacus being present due to a loss-of-life event. I know this won't always work, and it can't stop him from losing his own lives naturally as he grows up. But at least, with this shield, he won't accidentally be forced into other people's losses every day, and it will keep him safe from Abacus's reach just a little longer.

"Good job, Cian. Do you feel it around you? Think of it as your very own force field. I need you to promise me you'll keep up your shield every day, no matter what. You'll need to do it exactly as I showed you every morning," I say firmly, making sure he understands the importance.

"Of course, Aunt Clare, I promise," he says, agreeing without fully understanding that I'm trying to save his life.

I'll sleep easier knowing he can shield himself.

"Next, we'll work on fighting techniques and how to resist Abacus's pull. When you're older, I may even teach you how to beat him. But remember, you can never escape Fate. The best we can do is delay her."

"I love you, Aunt Clare!" Cian exclaims as he wraps his tiny arms around my waist, squeezing me with all his might.

His innocence makes me wish I had done things differently. I regret so many of my decisions.

"I can't wait to learn how to fight. I can be a hero and save the day with—" He pauses.

"Aunt Clare, what are you teaching me all of this for?" he asks, looking up at me with furrowed brows.

"I love you, my sweet boy. I'm teaching you how to defend yourself from the darkness in this world, and I pray to heaven you never need it." A tear rolls down my cheek as I close my eyes, trying to capture the moment with him before he has to leave me.

...

Had I known it would be the last time I'd see Cian, I would have told him everything—or perhaps I wouldn't have. A young boy has no use for weapons and research. His parents are keeping him from me, those ungrateful bastards. They're threatening to move if I try to see him again. I understand why Cian told them, but I wish he hadn't. They can't understand. The loneliness is more than I can bear.

The days drag on without Cian to brighten them with his curiosity and kindness. I have my affairs in order for what comes next. I'm leaving him my home, the money, all of my research, and a few surprises. I pour a glass of whiskey and go to find Shelby.

"It's almost time, I can feel it" I say to myself.

...

I have lived through countless horrors and seen more loss than most. I'm still haunted by my past, begging for this torment to cease. The dark day I betrayed my best friend, setting into motion the events that brought only pain and suffering into my world, started out innocent enough. We were happy and carefree. We'd just started a road trip with some college friends during spring break my freshman year—headed to the beaches in California for sun, boys, and underage drinking, or so we thought. I was overly confident in my ability to control everything, and it cost me everything.

Shelby had been my best friend since grade school. She knew how terrible my childhood was, and I swear her family fed me more than my guardians ever did. She was like a sister. Even though we were so close, I never told her the truth about me—about my abilities. I never trusted her enough, and that hurts me to this day because I missed the chance to let Shelby really know me.

We stopped to stretch our legs at Arizona's wonder of the world. Shelby and I started exploring, but we got overly confident and ignored the signs to stay on the trail. Deciding to go our own way, we hiked a more challenging route. We chanted "you only live once" loudly as we slid down the steep cliff, quickly losing sight of the car and our friends. Shelby was running down the trail like a natural with her long, gazelle-like legs, while I cautiously fell behind, trying to watch every step for possible hazards.

"Come on, Clare! Get a move on before I leave you behind! We're losing daylight!" Shelby yelled up to me.

"Okay, but you'll have to carry me back up when I break an ankle on these rocks and die!" I yelled back with a laugh, but I was fully serious, already calculating three hundred and forty-seven ways we could die out here.

I started recklessly running down the path to catch up with her, jumping over boulders like I was athletic—though I wasn't.

"Slow down! I can't keep up! Everything's a blur!" I shouted as I struggled.

I stepped right onto a snake's tail, and just as it was about to strike my leg, time stopped. I knew Abacus was appearing, signaling that the snake bite would cause a Loss event, which made sense given how long it would take for help to arrive and how venomous this snake was. I was going to die today.

Panic surged in my chest as I remembered I only had one life left. I'd used my second-to-last life to save a little girl who had been hit by a car last week. I didn't regret it, but I was so young and had so much I still wanted to do. I had never loved or been loved.

Abacus appeared beside the canyon, its impenetrable eyes locking onto mine. Before it could speak, I screamed out.

"No! Leave me alone, you monster! Go take someone else's life!"

I knew this was my last life, and I was terrified to go with Abacus. If I hadn't given away so many of my lives, I would still get to live. I was filled with regret and sorrow—bitter, sour sorrow. I wished to live, and as I spoke those words, a rush of power flowed through me. It took me by surprise because I wasn't trying to channel anything.

With only one life left, I thought Abacus would take me right then, but there was only silence as we stood there, frozen in time on the side of the massive canyon. Memories of my past played like an old movie in my mind—how I'd spent each of my nine lives, reliving them again. I'd had a tough childhood, and death was a constant presence before I learned how to shield myself. I'd given nearly all my lives to others, and now I would die for it.

Then, a blinding light radiated from the golden ring in Death's clutches. A second row appeared. I don't blink as I watch the new row glow red as if it were on fire. Both rows only have one life remaining, from what I can tell. Who could that second row belong to? I am in the middle of nowhere. Though Abacus has a limitless reach when it comes to collecting souls, my abilities I thought only touched those in my immediate area.

Before I can process what is happening, the red bead disappears, followed by Abacus. I close my eyes, and when I open them, I am alone again. I immediately look down, remembering the snake that had been about to bite my leg.

"Where did it go?" I mutter, searching around, assuming it is about to strike.

I am okay. The snake is gone, and I am still here. How? Relief washes over me, but so does immediate anxiety and fear. My luck had never been this good. If the snake left, what would kill me next?

I take a deep breath, overwhelmed with excitement that I am still alive and dread that the other shoe would drop shortly. I found myself ready to celebrate with Shelby. Though she won't know why I am so cheerful, I am certain she will go along with it. She always does. She is the best friend I could have ever asked for, has always had my back since we were kids.

"Woohoo!" I shout, thrilled to be alive.

I can't believe I am still here, and that Abacus just left like that. I don't understand what happened, but I don't want to jinx it. Who did that second row belong to? The question haunts me like a ghost.

I look down again to make sure I hadn't been mistaken, and the snake was still gone. I remember that Shelby had been hiking just ahead of me and probably heard my scream. I made my way to where I thought she was and called out.

"Hey, Shelby! Are you ready to celebrate!" No reply.

I climb down further and am hit with a nauseous feeling in my stomach. I see her lying in the rocks and dirt further down the cliff.

"Shelby!" I call out.

I see a snake slither away, disappearing into the rocks as I rush to her. I lift her limp body into my lap. Was that the same snake? It couldn't be. Her cold body lay in my arms, and the truth hits me like a wave. I did this. I had told Abacus to take someone else's life, and the closest living person was Shelby. I stole her last life instead of facing Fate. I had killed her. A cold chill runs up my spine, followed by a deep pain that causes me to cry out.

"Why!" I scream, my voice echoing across the canyon, making birds fly away.

"I'm so sorry, Shelby. It should be me. I love you. Please don't go!" I cry, embracing her as tears stream down my face, praying that she is in a better place now.

"Abacus! Please come back. Take me instead of her!" I beg, but I am met with silence.

We sat in the canyon for hours until our friends finally found us. I was a wreck, and I wouldn't release my grip on Shelby until the paramedics finally ripped me off of her. I dropped out of school the next day and withdrew from society.

I felt like I deserved to be dead. I killed my best friend, and with only one life left, I was on borrowed time.

I figured I would be dead by New Year's. I thought about ending it all to join Shelby, but I was a coward. I never followed through with it. I had to live with my sin, and it ate me up physically and mentally every day.

...

Many years later, with so many more lives ruined, I still remain. As I mentioned before, there is a price to pay for using these powers, and most can't afford it. Some have something worth dying for, but that was never me... until he came into my life. He changed everything and made me want to stop. I would have stopped for him. My love.

Fate had different plans. My once brown eyes are now cold blue, and my soul is nearly depleted. Most would envy eyes like these, but for me, they are a constant reminder of the day I first took a life. I can't undo what I've done, though I searched for decades, trying to find a way to make things right. I followed every fable, every ghost story, but I always end up in the same place: alive. I'll do everything I can to make sure Cian doesn't repeat my mistakes, that he is better than I was.

...

"Come on, Shelby, it's time for bed, girl! Where's that dog?" I call, searching the yard but unable to find her.

She never runs off and always loves bedtime, mostly because I let her sleep with me in the king-size bed. She's a blanket hog and loves to cuddle. The only things keeping me here are Cian and that dog.

"Treats!" I call out for her.

"Shelby, get in here now!" I say, starting to worry something has happened to her.

Was she hurt? Maybe she got into the trash again or was chasing that pesky raccoon living in the back shed. I close my robe and step outside, feeling the crisp breeze kiss my cheeks. The air feels stale, and everything around me quiets as I take another step into the yard.

Before I make it to the shed, I feel it. The pain in my chest is intense, and numbness spreads down my arm. A cold chill ran up my spine—almost as familiar as the scent of the lilacs I had planted near the shed. Abacus appears, standing before me, just as menacing as ever. I finally figured it all out.

"Are you ready?" Abacus asks.

"Yes." I answer, no longer scared but feeling confident that this is the right path.

"Thank you." I whispered, my last words as Abacus reached out to touch my shoulder signifying my end as a mortal.

"I love you Cian." My last words echo out.

CHAPTER 4
CIAN: THE GROUP

Years later, I find myself standing in an old library in Uptown Chicago, contemplating every decision I've made since age nine and wishing I had done so many things differently. But I do love this old building—the white stone has so much character. It makes me think of the stories Aunt Clare used to tell me about castles with gargoyle statues, knights, and dragons. She always said gargoyles were guardians sent from above to watch over us, promising me they would keep me safe if I needed them. It has always been a comforting thought.

I look down at the cup of coffee I just poured and hesitate for a second before taking a sip. I have no clue how long it has been sitting out or who made it, but it's coffee, so down the hatch. I scan the room, searching for her, but come up empty. I keep coming to these meetings mostly because of her, even though she hates me. With good reason.

"Hey, how has your week been?" Charlie asks.

"It was okay. Wish it was more interesting. I just stayed home and slept a lot." An anxious John answers, trying to make idle conversation before the meeting starts.

The group should be starting soon. Where is she? I always hide in the back because I hate small talk even more than I dislike being alone in my apartment with my thoughts. The idea that anyone actually wants to hear about my life is a foreign concept. I know I have issues and given my past, you would too. Besides, everyone here just looks at me like an adoration, their eyes filled with endless questions about Abacus and my abilities. I keep most of the details secret, or else they'd probably run away screaming.

This is our one-year anniversary, and of course, she doesn't show. There are only five of us, including me, and without her, everyone is going to talk to me the entire time. Maybe she's just running late, I reason with myself.

"Hi, Cian. Oh gosh, are you drinking that leftover coffee?"

"It's not the worst I've had," I respond, grunting so she knows I want to be left alone.

Charlie is great. She's kind and thoughtful enough to understand that my grunt means exactly what she thinks it does. She doesn't try to fix me or tell me how grunting like that makes me sound like a buffoon, like a certain someone would have. No, Charlie is sweet but for the life of me, I can't see myself dating her, even though she is classically beautiful and kind. She is so thoughtful as soon as she got a job with the city library, she found a way to move our meetings here and for free.

Too bad John won't man up and act on his crush on her. Charlie and John could be a cute couple, I suppose. She's always smiling and has this pleasant southern accent, while John is basically a recluse who would probably be scared of his own shadow if you told him, it was out to kill him. He never got past his first time meeting Abacus and is terrified to repeat the encounter. Eight lives left though, not bad.

Charlie is the kind of person who genuinely wants to get to know everyone and never forgets a birthday, which can be annoying but also kind of endearing. John is kind of the exact opposite of Charlie. He's always too focused on Abacus, documenting the group's Loss events, and trying to recruit more people like us from online chat groups. I keep telling him to stop with the chat groups before he gets in trouble. You never can trust someone online.

The door swings open, and my attention is immediately transfixed on her as she steps inside. If I thought there was any chance, she'd look my way, I'd stop staring, but she goes to extreme lengths to avoid even accidental eye contact with me. Once, she nearly got run over by a car because she saw me coming down the same side of the street and bolted across without looking. Thankfully, I was there to pull her to safety before Abacus showed up.

She makes her rounds, chatting with everyone in the group—everyone except me. She's hated me since the day we met. Inara James is the best part of this group, and the only reason I keep coming back—well, her and Vale, but for completely different reasons. If I'm being honest, those two saved me from myself that day. A year ago, I was in a dark place, and they pulled me back into the world. This group has been a way for me to interact with people in a controlled setting, which is good because, for the most part, I don't like people.

John, Vale, and Inara were the original members, forming the group back in high school after experiencing a shared Loss event that, somehow, they all remembered. They never give any details on that though, too scaring from what I have gathered. Charlie joined a few months after I first came. John met her in some online chat room about near-death experiences. I like to tease him, saying she probably thought he was a serial killer at first. But sure enough, she lost a life and started seeing flashes of it in her dreams. She even experiences déjà vu near one of her Loss spots. That is a place where you lost one of your nine lives. Most people don't even notice the subtle changes in weather or the goose bumps you might get when standing where a previous Loss occurred. Charlie was desperate for answers and said John was not the first person she spoke to about it, but was the least scary and crazy sounding.

"Cian, are you going to join us, or would you rather lurk in the shadows like usual?" Inara asks, taking a seat next to Vale.

I'm surprised she spoke to me—she normally acts like I don't exist. I wonder what's changed.

"I knew you liked me, sweetheart," I say, flashing my best smolder as I walk over to sit next to John.

Inara is as beautiful as she is frustrating, and that's saying something because she is hands down the most frustrating person I've ever met. She's been under my skin since the day I met her—and sometimes, I wish she were under my sheets.

...

That night we met started with me getting drunk and wandering aimlessly through the city looking for trouble. After my honorable discharge from the Marines, I somehow decided to move back to Chicago. A city this busy has its perks, but for a depressed, aimless veteran failing to adjust to civilian life, it's not the best place to be. I was shutting the world out—every time I let someone in, they die. I storm down a sidewalk on the Michigan Ave, buzzed from four or five beers—but who's counting? My father always used to say, whenever someone asked how many he'd had, "Only two—the first and the last." He'd laugh harder at his own joke than anyone else. Mom hated it, which somehow made it even funnier.

I head toward a bar across the street that I frequent because the staff are friendly and, most importantly, it's a hole in the wall with no other patrons. I need another drink before this buzz fades. As I glance up, admiring the city's famous architecture, Fate intervenes.

Without warning, she collides into me. Reflex takes over, and I automatically place my arms around her body and carry her a few more steps before stopping abruptly as she starts fighting me. She's a feisty one—before I even process what's happening, she pushes my arms off and falls to the ground.

"Are you serious? You oaf!" she yells, her voice dripping with fury. It's oddly intriguing. And, if I'm being honest, kind of attractive.

I look down to make eye contact with this disgruntled damsel and immediately feel something shift in my chest, snapping my full attention to the moment. I offer her my hand, but she pushes me away, and gets up on her own. She throws back her red hair to reveal the greenest eyes I've ever seen. My reaction is less than ideal—alcohol is doing most of the talking for me at this point.

"You don't have to be rude; you ran into me, sweetheart."

Before she speaks, her face contorts into the cutest expression—furious, indignant, completely unintimidated despite our size difference. She's relentless, verbally lashing me with elegant precision as she retrieves her purse. I barely even notice her friend standing nearby, watching the exchange through pink sunglasses.

"Look here," Inara snaps. "You assaulted me and acted like I was a bug on your windshield. Are you so self-absorbed that other people don't even register in your world?"

It's amusing how she acts like she's the one towering over me. She hasn't backed down an inch, maybe I should've just kept walking with her. Her friend, still watching, finally steps in, placing a hand on my chest. "You two have enough heat to make the sun jealous."

Before I can respond, she touches Inara's shoulder, calming her instantly. That surprises me. Inara looks at me with those green eyes, and my heart skips a beat. It's an unfamiliar feeling, but I chalk it up to the alcohol and move past it quickly.

"As if," Inara scoffs.

"This jerk belongs in a zoo with the rest of the monkeys. Let's go, Vale."

"Ouch, you wound me," I say with mock pain.

"Now that you've gotten that out of your system, let me buy you gorgeous ladies a drink." I nod toward the bar across the street.

To my relief, Vale laughs at the shift in conversation. Before Inara can refuse, she answers for both of them.

"We're in. Lead the way, soldier."

"Gladly." I reply, correcting her, "but first—I'm not a soldier. I'm a Marine. And before you ask, yes, I saw combat. No, I don't want to talk about it. You are very welcome."

I start toward the bar without looking back.

"Oh honey, I had no idea there was a difference," Vale teases.

"I'm Vale, by the way, and this magnificent woman you had the pleasure of running into is Inara." She winks.

"Pleasure to meet you both," I say, purposefully leaving out my name.

"And you are?" Inara presses.

"Need to know only," I reply, smirking as I keep walking.

"Ooh, mysterious," Vale muses, clearly checking me out.

"I'm not going in there with a guy who won't even tell us his name. Look at this place—are they even open?" Inara protests.

"I'll make you a deal," I say, turning to face them.

"Come inside, have a drink with me, and then I'll tell you, my name." I wink.

Vale whispers something to Inara and touches her arm. They exchange a look before nodding in agreement.

"Follow me, ladies," I say, opening the door.

"I hope you're ready for a treat."

"Let's do this," Vale says, taking my hand as I help her up the steps into the bar. Inara follows behind, begrudgingly.

"Are you going to apologize?" A very frustrated Inara snaps at me while I try to flag down the bartender.

"I have nothing to apologize for, sweetheart, but I see how you might feel that way. Running into a mountain can hurt, but that doesn't mean the mountain is wrong for existing," I say smugly, flexing my back and arms as I wave to the bartender again.

"Okay, ladies, what are you having?"

"I want a tequila and soda water, and she will have a whiskey and Coke with a lime," Vale answers, clearly trying to de-escalate the situation.

The place is busier than usual, making me a bit uneasy, but we get our drinks. I slam my shot and order another.

"So, what's your name? You made a deal, and we held up our end," Vale says, grabbing Inara's arm and whispering something I can't hear.

"Mi nombre es Cian, but you can call me anytime," I reply with a smirk and make sure to annunciate like they taught me in those two years of Spanish classes that I failed in High School.

"Is that supposed to be cute?" Inara scoffs, rolling her eyes.

A few drinks later, Inara finally starts to relax, but part of me enjoys seeing how flustered I can make her.

"Nice ink. Is that a dragon?" Inara asks after I catch her staring at my arms.

"It is, and before you ask, yes, I have more," I say, slamming another whiskey to keep sobriety at bay.

Vale touches my arm, and I can tell it annoys Inara. That thought alone brings me a sense of satisfaction. I make a show of pulling up my shirt, revealing the tattoo on my chest. I lock eyes with Inara, watching her gaze drift downward. Her cheeks flush a perfect shade of pink to match that fiery red hair. She's a sight to behold.

"Those look like they hurt," Vale says with a giggle.

I start thinking of my next move to get them back to my place, but Inara's dismissive behavior toward me is a distraction. I may not have my life together or be able to make it a day without drinking to dull my past, but this—this is something I've mastered.

"I can tell Vale is the fun one, and you, on the other hand, are already up past your bedtime," I say, keeping my eyes locked on Inara to watch her lose that tight grip on control.

"In your dreams. I'm just bored by you and this place. They aren't even playing music," she retorts.

To my surprise, she smirks, a small but undeniable sign of her wit. She's holding back, and I want to know why. It both intrigues and annoys me that I can't figure her out, yet.

"If you wanted music, all you had to do was ask sweetheart. They have karaoke in the corner; it just doesn't usually start until everyone is drunk. And if I bore you so much, why are you still here?" I say with a smile.

"The free drinks. Thanks. Bye." Inara quips before dashing away.

Vale runs after her. I know they're talking about me, but they're too far away for me to hear. I turn back to the bar, waving down the bartender for another round when suddenly, a sound cuts through the noise and immediately transports me away. Her voice is soft, velvet and soothing. The only thing more shocking than her hidden talent is her song choice—Let Her Go by Passenger. Each note swirls melancholy and woe inside of me. For the second time today, I have a cardiac event. She sings as if no one else is here, and I can tell she picked this song for herself. Goosebumps cover my arms, and I can't take my eyes off her. She is gorgeous.

...

"And you let her go," Inara finishes the song perfectly.

The entire bar erupts in cheers, snapping me back to reality and nearly makes me dive behind the bar for cover. For the first time in my life, I don't know what my next move is. This girl is amazing and keeps surprising me. She is different in the most frustrating and exciting way.

"What does a girl have to do to get a drink around here?" Inara asks as she walks back up and drums on the bar.

"Well, you could use those to get the bartender's attention," I say, gesturing to her chest with a cocky grin.

"That is crass. And your shirt is too small—makes it look like you're overcompensating for something," she snaps, making a hand gesture that implies exactly what she means.

"Sounds to me like you want to see for yourself. I have to admit; I was impressed by your song. I couldn't take my eyes off of you," I say, stepping close enough that she has to tilt her head to keep eye contact.

"Cian, could you please get us some more drinks?" Vale interrupts, wrapping an arm around Inara.

"I'm going to sign up for some Miranda and really get this party started," Vale says, dragging Inara toward the karaoke sign-up while I grab another round.

I don't need to work, between my early medical retirement from the Marines and Aunt Clare's inheritance, I'm set for life. Not that I touch that money. I only use it to maintain her house, though I haven't been there since before my last deployment. Too many bad memories. The night rolls on, full of dancing, laughter, and drinks. Eventually, it's closing time. Vale slid me her number when Inara was distracted by one of the singers so one down and one to go.

"If you ladies are up for it, we could head to my place for dessert," I say, raising an eyebrow.

This is going to be an epic night. Cian, you are the man. Two of the hottest girls are about to grace you with their presence all night, and you didn't even think about death once since meeting them. Well, almost.

"Are you kidding me? You're such a pig. You know, I actually thought you might be different for a moment. Thanks for proving me wrong," Inara snaps, storming off.

"Come on, Vale. He's not who we thought he was."

"Thanks again for the drinks. Bummer you can't stop thinking with your appendage long enough to make new friends. Thought you were fun to hang with, but you can lose my number." Vale says before leaving with Inara.

I don't try to stop them. I wouldn't even know what to say. I read those signals completely wrong.

"Fuck." I say under my breath and start to sober up a bit as the shame creeps in.

And I fucked that one up a bit sooner than normal.

...

I thought Inara was ridiculous for getting water at a bar, but little did I know, she was a genius. The next day, I didn't have a hangover and was sober before dawn. Looking back, she was fully justified in counting me out, and I regret not apologizing to her then. But at the time, I was in a different headspace—self-absorbed and more than a little reckless.

A week later, I drunk texted Vale and to my surprise she texted me, asking to hang out. She also told me to apologize for being a jerk. So, we went to lunch, but we immediately agreed that we should stick to just being friends. We have similar interests, and she has a dark, twisted sense of humor that matches mine. Almost every time we hang out, she brings Inara along, which I hate to admit I rather enjoy.

After a while, Vale tells me about their near-death experience group—a small gathering where they share stories of their encounters with death at their friend John's place. To their surprise, I reveal that I'm all too familiar with death myself. In fact, I even have a name for it.

"Abacus," I say, making a circle with my hands in the air.

"Because of the golden ring with counting beads it carries."

At first, I go to the group out of curiosity and boredom, but I stay for the feeling I get from sharing what I know. And, if I'm honest, I also stay because it gives me an excuse to be around Inara more, which I don't hate. This group reminds me of my old military unit. In some ways, the bonds they share ground me in a way I didn't realize I needed. I wonder if Aunt Clare ever had a group like this. A best friend to confide in.

None of them have my experience or my abilities—but they do remember bits and pieces of their losses. They remember Abacus and at least part of their deaths. They describe it like having half the puzzle pieces and knowing what the picture should look like, but never being able to put it together. John always says it's clear in his dreams, but when he wakes up, it's fragmented, like a bomb went off. And once he learned I had been in a few explosions myself, he always apologized after saying it.

But they aren't like me. No one is. I can use my lives to save people, to move during a Loss and who knows what else Aunt Clare never got the chance to teach me. Still, I feel a connection to them. Even though we started as strangers, they understand this part of me that I have to hide from the rest of the world. Here, I can actually be myself. My true self. Not just the shell of a man everyone else expects me to be.

I know what I look like to most people—a tall, muscular veteran with scars and tattoos. They take one look at me and think they already know my story. But no one knows the full story.

When people see a Marine vet, they usually thank me for my service or tell me how close they came to joining when they were younger—always followed by some plausible reason why they didn't. I never ask, but they always tell me. Maybe they feel like they need to justify themselves. But I don't judge those who didn't serve. They're the reason I did.

This group is different. They never make me feel like I have to be anything but myself. They let me be a grumpy, used-up vet with too much anger and time on his hands. One night after a meeting, Vale mentioned that Inara's favorite band was playing down the street, so I bought tickets for the whole group on a whim. We had a great time. Inara, of course, was unimpressed that I paid for pit tickets and pulled some strings with security to get us backstage. Little does she know I did it entirely for her.

My first meeting with the group, though—that was a train wreck. John's mom answered the door with a warm smile and welcomed me inside. I wasn't prepared for the hug that followed, but I guess there are worse ways to be greeted. She led me downstairs, holding my arm "just in case I fell," she justified.

John lives at home with his parents, in their partially finished basement. He's exactly what you'd expect from a college dropout who trades stocks online for a living. Apparently, he makes decent money, but after meeting Abacus a few years ago, he prefers to stay off the grid.

That said, John is also the kind of guy who would give you the shirt off his back if you needed it. When he lost his first life, it changed him. Now, he's afraid of... well, everything.

We aren't meant to remember a Loss for a reason. Abacus is menacing, and recalling your own death without any other context would drive anyone mad. People die every day from the most ordinary things—things we don't even register as risks. A walk across the street could end with a car accident. A simple trip down the stairs, a slip in the shower. One hundred fifty people die every second worldwide, and that's not even counting those who use a life to not die.

John's basement was cramped, all four of us squeezed onto an old orange couch that looked like it had been left behind in the seventies. It felt like sandpaper against any exposed skin. Once I told them my secret, they had questions—so many questions. John and Vale wanted to know everything, so I started with the basics.

"You know the old saying, 'A cat has nine lives? Well, that actually got twisted over time. We're the ones with nine lives," I explain, diving into the history and what I know about Abacus.

I can't deny it—it feels good to hold their attention, to be needed again. They genuinely want to learn from me, so I oblige. I leave out the stuff about Fate being a control freak that will show up if things get to far from the plan and I don't mention the old stories Aunt Clare told me about angels and some great war for all life. They already think I am crazy enough without adding more fuel to the fire. I can see them admitting me on the spot if I told them all my secrets.

"We're all born with exactly nine lives," I continue.

"Some people lose each life one by one over a lifetime in a single Loss event, while others experience a total Loss event that takes as many lives as they have remaining all at one time. Those are rare. Those are moments when someone decides they are ready to punch out early and say; yes."

"Wait, what?" John asks.

"We can choose?" Vale echoed, her brows knitting together.

I hesitated, then told them about Cruz—how he had said yes right in front of me before I could stop him. I hate to admit it, but I had missed this; having people to talk to, to share life with. I'd been tucked away in my own world for so long that I had forgotten what it was like.

"The catch to all this," I said, "is that you're not supposed to remember. Most people spend their nine lives without ever realizing it. But not us. Statistically, we'll use them all up before we turn forty, at least according to my aunt."

The small, drafty basement suddenly feels like a classroom, and I am the teacher.

I do my best to share what I know without terrifying them, but I need them to understand the dangers. They have to be ready because Abacus is always ready for us.

"What do you call it when everything stops, and Abacus shows up?" Vale asks.

"I call it a Loss. It is like a limbo between realms and is outside of time and space. I remember something about the Void too but not enough to be helpful." I say, shrugging.

"Aunt Clare and I never really finished talking through all of this. In her defense, it wasn't the most important thing for me to learn with the limited time we had."

That gets a few head nods of agreement out of them. Inara was the one who spoke next.

"It's like an out-of-body experience," she says.

"Your life flashes before your eyes. I like the name Abacus for that creepy presence that's always there. Some research suggests it changes form—a child, a woman, a man—whatever makes the experience easier for the person being reaped or maybe to make you the most creeped out."

John cracked open a can of Mountain Dew from his ever-present backpack, taking a sip before asking, "Are those moments… outside of time?"

"Yes. When a Loss happens, the world freezes—well, mostly everyone." I laugh at the absurdity of my own words.

Realizing just how abnormal I am.

…

Now, what about you? Have you ever slipped in the shower? Maybe tripped down the stairs but caught yourself at the last second? Nearly been hit by a car? Did you feel a strange twinge in your chest afterward? Or moment of dizzy recognition? Maybe you broke out in a cold sweat, struggled to catch your breath?

You might have already spent a life and never even realized it. Some people remember bits and pieces of Abacus. A rare few—like me—remember everything. Abacus has gone by many names throughout history—The Grim Reaper, The Boogeyman, Death, La Muerte. It comes without warning and wears whatever skin it wants. I don't know why it bothers, but I suppose it's better than a black-robed skeleton. Now, Abacus as a child, that was unsettling. Harder to ignore. Harder to hide as I watched the boy reap my Marines.

The one sure fire way to know you are facing off against Death is that it always has the Abacus. In my life time at least, it is always a golden ring with abacus beads on one life line. My aunt told me he never takes the same form twice, as if searching for the perfect fit but never quite finding it. For those unfamiliar, an abacus is an ancient counting tool which came before calculators. But in this case, the beads count something else: your lives.

Aunt Clare believed each row of beads represented a single life. Normally, only one row would appear during a

Loss. But for people like me—those who've shared a Loss—you could see more than just your own. I am getting off track. I seem to do that a lot.

...

"I think I'm ready to share my Loss," John says breaking me from my thoughts.

The entire group fell silent. John had never shared his story—not once since the group had formed. He had always been beyond careful, avoiding another Loss at all costs. Even I was curious to hear what he had to say.

"This one was different," he admitted, exhaling slowly, staring at his hands.

"Afterward, I still felt it. I can still feel the glass cutting into my skin, the blood spraying everywhere."

Charlie gasps, moving closer to pat his back, her chair made a loud screech as she did.

"I stepped into the shower and instantly felt the chill run up my spine. Before my other foot even hit the floor, déjà vu washed over me. And then... I saw him. Standing there. Watching me."

John's voice drops lower, and for the first time, I saw understanding in his eyes; the kind of understanding I wished he didn't have.

"I slipped. I hit my head on the glass shower door. And boom, there he was. Abacus. Asking me if I was ready. Before I even realized it, the answer came out of my mouth. Then suddenly, I was catching myself, gasping, water hitting me in the face instead of…" He trailed off, shaking his head.

"I don't know if I can keep going if this nightmare doesn't stop replaying in my head," he admitted with a nervous laugh.

"Does anyone know how to stop it?"

Silence. Everyone was in shock.

I remember something Aunt Clare had told me once, buried deep in her stories. If only she were still here… But no good came from walking down dead ends. John had shared something painful, and I should say something—let him know he wasn't alone.

"Good share, John. And don't worry. Those nightmares should fade over time, but maybe switch to baths for a while." I say trying to cut the tension.

The group chuckled, but something was gnawing at me. A memory just out of reach. Then it hit me.

"I remember. It's called a Death Loop."

John paled and everyone stares at me. I hadn't meant to say that out loud. A Death Loop—when someone is stuck in the same nightmare, reliving the way they lost their past life and if it is not stopped, they will lose all of their remaining lives that way. It typically consumes you and becomes a self-fulfilling prophecy.

"What does that mean for him?" Charlie asks, concern written all over her face.

I hesitate. "Nothing," I lie.

"It's just a term my aunt came up with for when someone keeps reliving a loss. Nothing to worry about. You will get past it in no time."

There is no point in scaring them when they can't do anything to stop it. I can, maybe. How would I even do that? In theory, it could work if I am near him when Abacus shows up. I could either give him one of my lives so he still has one left after losing his last seven or better yet I can just stop him from dying and losing another life in the shower. John walks over to me, and before I can dodge him, he wraps his arms around me in a hug.

"Okay, man. It'll all be alright," I say, slipping out of the embrace before it gets any more awkward.

"Remember you are a bath guy now." I say with a smirk and try to lighten the mood.

I quickly move the conversation onto trying to resist answering Abacus hoping they don't ask any more questions about Death Loops. Especially because I am out of answers at the moment.

"Has anyone been able to say anything except no in a Loss?" I ask.

"I barely remember losing the life, but I don't think I would try to even if I could. Abacus terrifies me." Charlie says as she covers her face with her hands.

"I would most certainly have a long list of questions for Abacus should I find that I could say anything other than, no." Inara chimes in and elbows Vale as if they were having a secret conversation the rest of us could not hear.

Vale once told me she tried her hardest not to answer Abacus's question, but after what felt like only a second, Abacus repeated it louder—pulling the words from her throat. I've seen it happen, even tried to fight it myself overseas, when I thought maybe my rifle could end Abacus. As if a weapon could hurt death. The more you fight the urge to answer, the more aggressive Abacus becomes, and who knows what kind of power it could wield if it ever got angry enough.

We've all spent more time together than apart this past year, and somehow, I am feeling again. It's a lot better than the numb jerk I was a year ago. I am starting to feel like this is my new family, except Inara still makes my blood boil. She's stubborn, outspoken, frustratingly beautiful— I might have a problem. How did I not see this sooner?

I catch myself staring at her while she talks to Vale. She looks different today, but I can't place why. I rock back in my chair, trying to push away the anxiety clawing at my gut. There's a shadow over her today, a weight I can feel from across the room. Before I can finish the thought, she stands.

"I died." she says and brings the room to a pause waiting for her next words.

The pain in her voice makes my stomach twist. I swear I see a tear before she blinks it back. This means she is down to five now. A sick part of me feels relief, a twisted sense of connection to her through our losses. The guilt that follows is instant and crushing. I look away, trying to pull myself together. She starts to share with the group, and I can see the experience rattled her more than she's willing to admit.

"I was walking Spencer, as usual," she says.

"I remember saying hi to my neighbor Phil, who was crossing the street. Then I heard screeching tires—turned just in time to see it coming. The next thing I knew, everything went cold, and Abacus was there."

Her voice drops into something eerily familiar, and the words send a chill up my spine.

"Are you ready?"

Each memory of Abacus floods my mind, shaking loose questions I thought I had already answered.

"I don't even remember saying anything," she continues.

"The next thing I know, Spencer is pulling me out of the way as the car crashes feet away from us." She exhales and sinks back into her seat, exhausted from reliving it.

"I am going to put you in a big plastic bubble. I can't stand the thought of losing you," Charlie says and proceeds to give Inara a surprise hug that constricts her airflow.

"I think I saw your loss," Vale whispers, then clams up.

I could almost pretend I didn't hear it

"Inara, let me know if there's anything I can do. I get how hard this is," John says, glancing at me like he's checking to make sure I agree and shifting my focus from Vale's comment, for now.

I just sit there, arms crossed, avoiding eye contact. I fail miserably. I spend the next hour doing nothing but stealing glances at her, my gaze lingering too long on those piercing green eyes. When the meeting finally winds down, Inara grabs John's arm.

"I have to get home. Spencer still needs dinner. See you next week," she says.

"So soon?" John asks. "Okay, but after next meeting, we should all grab drinks."

"Drive safe. Give that chocolate fur baby belly rubs from me," Charlie says, hugging her.

Jealousy rises in my throat like bile. I clear my throat, scrambling for something to say as she passes me.

"See you later, bro," I say.

What the hell was that? Did I just have a stroke? She doesn't even dignify it with a response. Just rolls her eyes and moves on to hug Vale goodbye. I watch her hips sway as she walks to the door, her skirt hugging her curvy frame just right. I bite my lip, watching her go, replaying every second of the past year where I could have been something—anything—other than her biggest annoyance.

Everyone else says normal things like "bye" or "drive safe." Not me. I say, "Later, bro."

The sweet scent of her perfume lingers in the air, triggering memories like landmines. The first night I met her, standing under dim bar lights, singing into a microphone, her voice wrapping around me like a spell. Another night—her putting up her hair, curled up with a book while rain kept us inside. We were supposed to go swimming that day, but lightning canceled the plans. Vale insisted I stay anyway, and I was glad I did. Inara cooked us pasta that night, and I haven't stopped thinking about it since.

"Fuck," I mutter under my breath.

I have feelings for Inara. And I just spent the past year feuding with her like a damn Montague vs Capulet. I take a deep breath, trying to clear my head, but something about today feels different. I can't wait until next week to see her again. Every second since she walked out tightens a noose around my neck. Why do I find her so intoxicating? I don't know what kind of hold she has on me, but I can't shake it. She drives me crazy every time we speak. She's the most frustratingly beautiful woman I've ever met, and she makes me want to be better.

I once watched her chase down a stray dog for four blocks after karaoke, determined to get it to safety. Said she didn't want the fur baby to get hurt, but it is just her heart. Maybe it's because I'm finally ready to face my feelings, and maybe it's the fact that she's down to five lives too, but I have to act. I push back my chair and make for the door.

John shouts something behind me—something about a fire—but I'm already outside, moving.

"Inara!" I call out, catching her just before she reaches her car.

She turns, surprised, and before I can second-guess myself, I march up to her and grab her by the waist then pull her close. This is the closest we've been since the day we met. I don't ask permission but the look her eyes gives her away. I kiss her, unapologetic, with a year of bottled-up desire finally breaking free.

CHAPTER 5
INARA: APOLOGY ACCEPTED... EVENTUALLY

Who does this guy think he is? Look at him—his arms around me like they belong there, staring into my eyes with those pools of golden caramel I just want to dive into, as if he isn't assaulting me right now. His dumb, chiseled face and infuriating power over me are so surprisingly hot and confusing that I am partially in shock. He thinks he can just kiss me after a year of ignoring my existence. What a dick.

What a completely unexpected and delicious thing he is doing to me. I can feel him pressing into me, and if he weren't holding me in place, I might melt from all this heat. No. He can't just act like I'm his. He can't pick me up in his strong arms and kiss me like I belong to him. He's never— Not even once— For an entire year—

Cian is overly confident and the most frustrating man I have ever met, but his body is ridiculous, and I have thought about this moment more than a few times. He is most certainly a man. Ugh. I feel things I don't want to feel, and I should make him stop. Why am I not making him stop? Because you don't want him to, Inara. And you're suddenly very thankful you had no onions on your salad earlier today.

If Vale hadn't befriended this jerk, I would've been rid of his gorgeous amber eyes and firm ass long ago. But typical Vale, bringing home strays. His eyes are so warm and inviting. They remind me of my childhood summers on the family farm—the way the sun lit up the fields just right, turning them into a sea of gold.

He has no right to touch me. I should slap him right across his perfect face. Would serve him right. His tongue seduces my mouth without warning, and I don't know if I should bite it or give in to the intense desire to kiss him back. My lips seem to be on autopilot, pressing tight against his. A breath of anger wells inside me, and I bite down.

Finally, I find the will push him off. His muscular chest absorbs the blow so effortlessly that he doesn't even move an inch. He laughs. That smug bastard. Lowering me to the ground like I weigh nothing—like I didn't just bite his tongue—he grins.

"No need to be so violent, sweetheart. I would have stopped sooner, but your body was telling me to keep going, so I gladly did. That was the best kiss of my life."

That smug, handsome face has me spinning.

"Why are you smiling?!" I demand, rage bubbling up.

"Why did you just kiss me? You have no right to touch me!" I hit his shoulder with a right hook my uncle taught me.

My hand hurts and he doesn't even wince.

"Good form."

To my surprise, he steps back. Hands up. Head bowed.

"Inara, I am so sorry. I know it's a year late, but you deserve an apology. I want you to know how I feel about you. You're all I think about. You're the biggest reason I still come to this group. You are the best part of my week, and I don't want to stand in my own way any longer. Please, forgive me."

My jaw drops. I probably look like a bass fish. For a full minute, I can't speak. I can't process what's happening. I thought Cian hated me. I thought he ignored my existence as some twisted way of messing with me. I think back to the kiss, to those arms pulling me tight against his firm body, holding me. My cheeks burn as a warm sensation flows through me, washing away my anger and replacing it with emotions I've spent the last year suppressing out of self-preservation.

I've not felt his muscles since the night he plowed into me like a buffoon. But now? After being pressed against him like that? I can't help but picture him with fewer clothes. I watched him in group hanging out with Vale. And though I'd never admit this to anyone—not even Vale—I have thought about him romantically.

"Inara, I truly am sorry," he says, voice steady, eyes gleaming with something I've never seen before.

"I don't deserve your forgiveness, but I'm asking for it. And if you're not ready, I understand. I'll earn it. I'm patient when I want to be. And for you, I will be."

He steps back again, giving me space.

"You had no right to kiss me!" I snap, but the heat in my voice falters when I make the mistake of looking into his eyes.

God, those eyes. Tawny, deep, all-consuming. Like he can see right through my hard exterior—to the girl trapped inside who has no clue what to do right now. He never looked at me like this before. But I don't hate it.

"I do not forgive you. You don't just get to say 'I'm sorry' after a year of ignoring me and act like everything is fine between us. And that kiss—" I narrow my eyes.

"That was assault. Try it again, and I'll have you arrested!"

I stand there, locked in an inner battle between my desire and the overwhelming urge to cause him physical pain. I can't give in to this foolish notion that he's changed. Just last week, he was still the same arrogant jerk he's always been. No, this is a performance. And if I let him in, he'll hurt me, like they always do.

"I accept."

He says it with a smile before pressing a soft kiss to my hand. I yank it away from his rough, calloused grip.

"Accept what?" My voice drips with annoyance, and I know my expression matches.

"I accept your challenge, of course." He winks. "I'm patient enough to wait for you to come to terms with the truth."

"I didn't challenge you, and I know exactly what I want, Cian. And it is not you."

I spin toward my car, every part of me on high alert. He both disgusts me and turns me on, and I want to scream from the contradiction. Cian has so much confidence—it's maddening and attractive at the same time. And the way he saunters over and stops me from leaving makes my breath hitch. Why do I want to throw myself into his arms and kiss him again? The force pulling me toward him is unbearable, even as I fight it with everything I have.

"Leave me alone!" I finally snap, regaining enough composure to open my car door.

"I have to get home to feed Spencer. Goodbye, Cian."

He raises his hands in surrender and takes a slow step back, but not without leaving me with a parting shot.

"Don't count me out just yet, beautiful. I promise I'm not the guy you think I am."

Damn it. Why did he have to say that? And why does his voice have to sound like sin wrapped in honey? Once safely inside my car, I grip the steering wheel like a lifeline and pull away, needing space—privacy—to process the storm of emotions raging inside me. This man is infuriating. And yet, I already want to forgive him. By the time I get home, my head is still spinning.

Spencer, my tiny, scrappy, half-miniature pinscher, half-chihuahua, yips excitedly as I scoop his small body into my arms. He's been with me for years now, ever since I rescued him from a guy selling puppies at the swap meet.

"You, my chocolate baby, are the only man I need in my life."

I set him down and head for the shower, craving the kind of scalding heat that can wash away this entire day—this entire week. The second I step under the hot spray; my thoughts betray me. I feel Cian's arms around me, his intoxicating scent wrapping around my senses. I bite my lip, my fingers itching to run through his messy brown hair. His body was so firm, so strong.

It's not fair that he can eat an entire bag of gummy bears every week at group meetings and never gain a single pound. Meanwhile, I just think about a gummy bear, and my jeans get tighter. I groan, pressing my forehead against the cool tile. I don't need this. Not today. Not with everything else going on. Losing a life while walking Spencer was hard enough. Then the rejection letter from law school arrived—the one that called me an "impressive applicant" but said my application "lacked depth."

Whatever the hell that means. I finish my shower, pull on my softest pajamas, and climb into bed. Spencer curls up against my side as I grab my newest book, ready to lose myself in someone else's story. Then my phone buzzes. A text. From Cian. The surprise sends an unwelcome jolt through me. I don't have to read it. I won't read it. I toss my phone to the other side of the bed, willing myself to ignore it. He doesn't deserve my attention. He's a jerk. End of story.

Ding!

Another message. Maybe it's Vale this time. We text almost every day, so it's logical to assume it's her. Seconds pass. My heartbeat quickens. Curiosity gets the best of me. With a frustrated groan, I nearly dive across the bed, grabbing my phone to check the messages. Unfortunately for me, it's not Vale.

Cian: *Hi Inara, I just wanted to apologize again and say that you have the most beautiful green eyes I've ever seen.*
Cian: *Please let me make it up to you this Friday. I want to take you out. Let's say 7 p.m.? I'll pick you up at your place.*

"Ugh." I let out my frustration.

He didn't even ask, just assumed I would say yes. What a cocky asshole. But damn it... I do want to say yes. And he didn't even tell me where we're going, which annoys me. Now I have no idea how to dress. I hate surprises, especially when I can't figure them out ahead of time. Sure, I've been told I can act surprised well enough to win an Oscar, but that doesn't mean I enjoy it.

Inara: *Ok.*

I don't know why I just sent that. It's like I am possessed. He's been a jerk. He's not even that cute. Okay, maybe a little. And besides, there's that guy at the gym I've been low-key eyeing, but he's no Cian. He hasn't made my entire body feel like it's floating—like I could just disappear in the moment.

That kiss. Vivid, consuming, as if it had just happened all over again. His lips were soft, gentle, yet firm and have clearly made me lose my thin grasp on reality.

Inara: *Where are you planning on taking me? I assume somewhere without witnesses so you can murder me because you've actually been a serial killer this whole time and just pretended to be our friend.*

I might watch too many crime TV shows. Though I can vividly see this going down as the worst time of my life. Possibly even the end of my nine lives.

Cian: *It's a surprise.*
Cian: *Don't worry, I promise not to murder you. Dress in whatever makes you feel the most yourself.*

There's a possibility this might go well. Against all logic, I let myself feel the tiniest spark of excitement. His texts are... surprising. Sweet, even. I never let myself see him as anything other than the cocky, arrogant flirt he was the first night he met us. And yet, here I am. Considering a date with Cian.

I let out an involuntary screech and fall back on my bed, clutching my phone to my chest as a mix of emotions crash over me. The next thing I know, I awake to the sun shining in my bedroom and the sound of Spencer noisily pushing his food bowl across the wood floor in the kitchen.

I groan. "You know, some dogs let their owners sleep in."

He stares at me expectantly from the doorway, tail wagging. With a sigh, I roll out of bed. I need to get ready anyway—tonight is important. The gallery is hosting a new artist's exhibit, and for once, I am leading it. I need this to go perfectly to prove to Peggy that I have what it takes to run this place. She always talks about leaving the gallery to someone talented and trustworthy before she takes off to travel the world, searching for new art. That someone needs to be me. As I pour Spencer's food, my gaze flickers to my phone. A notification. A text.

Cian: *Goodnight, sweetheart.*

I smile—uncontrollably. Okay. Yeah. I definitely want to see him Friday. Date. Oh, God. I'm going on a date with Cian. I don't think I would've believed it a week ago. And while I'm still annoyed that he won't tell me where we're going, I realize… I kind of like the mystery. Vale knows me too well to ever let a surprise actually be a surprise. But with Cian, I have no idea what to expect. And that excites me.

…

At the gallery, Vale and I work together to set up for the exhibit while I spill everything from last night. She isn't even remotely shocked.

"When Cian kissed me yesterday…" I hesitate, still processing.

"And when I agreed to go out with him this Friday—"

Vale's expression is pure I told you so. "Inara, you're beautiful, smart, and the kindest person I know. Of course, Cian is into you."

I scoff. "Then why did he never—"

"How was it, by the way?" she asks, rolling her eyes like this is obvious.

I pause. The tension between Cian and me—was it ever really about anger? Or was it always attraction disguised as something else? Had I been in denial this entire time?

"…Kissing him was better than that chocolate cake at your favorite spot downtown," I admit.

Vale's jaw drops. "No way."

I nod. "I was conflicted, though. Part of me hated it. Wanted it to end. But the other part…" I trail off, shaking my head.

"The other part wanted more."

Vale watches me carefully, then crosses her arms.

"So, what's the problem?"

I sigh, adjusting a framed piece on the wall.

"Cian is probably just playing a game with me. Or he'll lose interest once he gets what he really wants, right?"

My fingers fidget with the hem of my shirt.

"If he hurts you in any way, I promise you it'll be the last thing he ever does," Vale says, deadly serious.

I grin despite myself. I love her so much.

"Not that it matters," I mutter.

"He's probably going to cancel anyway."

I don't know why I care so much. Actually... I don't know the last time I cared this much about a date.

"Hi, Peggy!" Vale practically shouts, and I turn to see our boss approaching.

That's my cue—time to push this conversation way down until later.

Vale has been extra nice to Peggy all week, hoping it will help her art career, but Peggy hates suck-ups almost as much as she hates talentless artists. She is exactly what you'd imagine a single, middle-aged woman running an art gallery to be—short jet-black hair, eccentric clothing, glasses. She poured everything she inherited into this place after her second husband died mysteriously. Since then, the gallery has been her entire life. No children, no real passions beyond discovering the next big artist before anyone else.

"Did you hear about the huge accident on the ninety-four?" Peggy asks, her tone unusually somber.

"No, what happened?" Vale asks.

"A semi crashed into nine cars on the highway. There were pieces of plastic and metal everywhere. The news reported twenty-three people died, including the driver of the sixteen-wheeler," Peggy says while trying to mask the grief on her face.

"That's awful. All those people..." I press a hand to my mouth, swallowing down intrusive thoughts.

"Needless to say, we have a busy day girls. Time to get back to work." Peggy turns and heads to her office.

"Inara, don't worry. We'll get you ready for that date," Vale says, nudging me.

"And trust me, Cian isn't half as bad as you think."

...

The highway tragedy haunts me for the rest of the week, chasing me like a storm cloud straight out of a cartoon. All those people—taken by Abacus. The thought sends a chill through me. I know people die every day, and highway accidents are nothing new with how reckless drivers are, but something about this one doesn't sit right. Twenty-three dead. Not one survivor. The odds of that have to be astronomical. Not that I can exactly call up Abacus to fact-check. Vale is running late today, and I have my date with Cian tonight. When she finally arrives, she's carrying a painting, moving cautiously, as if she's smuggling contraband.

"Wait… is that one of your paintings?" I ask, louder than I intended.

"Shh! I don't want Peggy to see it yet." Vale glances over her shoulder.

"I painted it after the accident." She hurries toward the empty wall Peggy reserved for the next display.

"You're hoping Peggy will showcase it at the next show." I cross my arms.

"You know she doesn't do favors. She'll see this as a favor."

"She won't if she thinks you brought it in. Tell her it's from a local artist you found. Please?" Vale gives me a cheesy grin I can't say no to.

"Fine," I sigh.

"But let me see it first."

She unwraps the painting and steps back, watching my reaction. It's incredible. Vale's talent is undeniable, and I have no doubt Peggy will love it. I just have to sell the lie first.

"I love it," I tell her honestly.

"The colors, the chaotic brushstrokes—it makes me feel like I was there. And that shadowy figure in the center... it reminds me of someone, but I can't place it yet. There's so much death and pain." I pause, narrowing my eyes.

"Vale... is that Abacus?"

Something about the painting tugs at something deep inside me. I don't know if I like that. Peggy is meticulous in selecting artists, sometimes taking months—years—to find one she deems worthy. She will not be happy that I'm stepping on her toes, even if Vale's work is undeniably brilliant.

"Girls, I'm heading out to meet some young artist in Pilsen. Apparently, he only paints in shades of orange using his—" Peggy stops mid-sentence, her gaze locking onto Vale's painting.

"What is this?" she asks, practically jumping out of her skin.

"I thought you might like it," I say, keeping my voice steady.

"It's from a gifted artist I found locally." Fingers crossed.

Peggy steps closer, her eyes scanning the canvas. "I need to meet this artist. Set up a meeting tonight at eight."

I swallow. "Actually, they're here now... if that's okay?"

I glance at Vale, and Peggy follows my gaze.

"You did this?" Peggy's voice is unreadable as she turns to Vale.

Vale stiffens but nods. If Peggy doesn't say something soon, she might lose her nerve entirely. And with Peggy's track record of firing people on a whim, this could be the last time either of us step foot in this gallery.

"Peggy, I asked Vale to bring it in. I thought we could showcase local talent, and who better than—"

"Hold it!" Peggy throws up a finger, silencing me.

She's thinking. That's a good sign. Peggy never wastes time on art that doesn't move her.

"Vale... you're fired. Inara, you too."

My stomach drops.

"I'm so sorry, Peggy, this was all my fault. Inara didn't—"

"I feel your pain in this piece," Peggy interrupts, still staring at the painting.

"How long have you two been hiding these talents from me?"

Vale looks like she might faint.

"I've been painting most of my life," she finally says.

"But this one… this one came out of me after the accident. I had to paint it." She grabs my hand, squeezing it so tight I almost yelp.

Peggy finally looks at us.

"You're both re-hired—on one condition. I get exclusive rights to sell your work here." She shifts her gaze to me.

"And Inara, you'll be the new gallery manager."

Vale's jaw practically unhinges.

"We accept," I blurt out, shaking Peggy's hand before she changes her mind.

This is it. Vale's big debut—her art, out for the whole city to see. And I get to manage the whole thing. Vale blinks at Peggy in shock.

"What she said," she stammers, before launching herself at Peggy in a hug.

Peggy stiffens like she's just been touched by a plague victim. Vale pulls back.

"Wait… you really like it?"

Peggy glares at her.

"Do you hate me, Vale?"

"What? No, of course, not—"

"Then why insult me so? Have I ever lied to one of my artists before? No!" Peggy gives me a wink, then turns back to Vale.

"I need more. Bring me everything you have tonight. If it's as good as this, we will have an entire showcase of your work."

Vale hesitates, until I give her a nudge.

"I have at least a dozen more," she blurts out.

"One I just finished this morning—it's even more raw than this one."

Peggy nods, satisfied.

"Then it's decided. You'll be our center focus and fill the entire west section of the gallery. You get thirty-five percent of any sales." She turns to me.

"And, Inara, if this goes well, you keep your promotion. If nothing sells..." She pauses for effect.

"You're both fired."

With that, Peggy walks away. Vale and I exchange glances. We have a hell of a lot of work to do.

"Cheer up, ladies. If her other work is half as good as this one, you have nothing to worry about," Peggy says over her shoulder before walking out the door into the bustling and windy streets of Chicago.

That woman has so much personality, I sometimes feel like I'm living in a TV show. You never really know where you stand with Peggy—especially when it comes to art. Or anything, really. I've seen her sell a painting for fifty grand more than she paid for it, only to cancel the artist's next show because one of their new pieces "irked" her. She said they lost it—whatever it is.

"Don't worry, Vale. I'll buy a few myself to save our jobs if it comes to that," I say, trying to comfort her.

She looks like she's starting to second-guess her bold move today. I love this job. And I love Vale's art—almost as much as I love reading. In another life, I'd be an agent at a major publisher or maybe a journalist, that is if I couldn't be a billionaire. According to my family, I have an unhealthy relationship with books, but they can get over it.

"I love you. You know that, right, Inara?" Vale says, interrupting my runaway thoughts and giving me the tightest hug ever.

"I love you too. And we got this." I hug her back.

I wish I knew more about how Vale paints her pieces, but she swears her mojo only works when she's alone. She once told the group that she paints what she remembers from her lost lives and from the different forms Abacus takes. But she hasn't lost a life in months—and this piece is so raw, so familiar—I know she's hiding something. I wish she trusted me enough to share it, but I wouldn't be much of a best friend if I didn't respect her privacy. I just have to trust she'll tell me when she's ready.

CHAPTER 6
ABACUS: UNRAVELING

"Are you ready?"

She just stares at me, blank expression frozen on her face. If she doesn't answer soon, I'm going to lose my patience. The list never ends, and the pressure to reap the next soul grows stronger by the second. Come to think of it, I don't remember anything before this moment. I only know that I am responsible for death—for tracking humanity's lives. I account for the time they wish to use, reset the cycle, or take them to the next realm. Have I done this so many times that I've been living in a fog? Strange. I don't even remember my name—or how long I've been doing this.

"Are you ready?" I ask again, because I know that's what I'm supposed to do.

I expect to force an answer out of her so I can move on to the next name on the list. But something feels different. My mind starts drifting, weighing the consequences of simply reaping her now versus delaying to explore this feeling. No—I could never do that. She has to answer. I'll ask again, this time with a bit more persuasion.

"Beth, I know this is scary, but you still have lives left. You could have many years ahead of you. Just answer the question so I may be done here," I say, and the words surprise me.

I meant to follow the script, but I can't seem to shut off these feelings. The pressure to complete the list keeps building, and the pain of staying in one place too long gnaws at me. Feelings, again. Why am I feeling? Death has no soul, no emotions—so why do I? I gaze into her eyes and see her fear—and an unfamiliar wave crashes over me. Is this empathy? Why isn't she answering? And why don't I know who I am? I feel the Void pulling me back. If I don't collect her soul soon, I might miss the window. That would be catastrophic. Do your job.

The terrified woman, clutching a bag of groceries, finally frees me from this place with a single word: "No."

Before she can blink, I collect one of her lives, mark it on my ring, and reset her. She's back in the parking lot, groceries in hand, just as the truck that hit her now narrowly misses. She remembers nothing. There's no trace of our exchange. I'm the only thing standing between this world and the next. So why do I feel like I just did something wrong? Maybe I need a break. I don't think I've ever taken one. Then again, I honestly can't recall anything before now, so how would I know?

As I shift back into the Void—a place outside of time and space that belongs to me alone—I feel a tug in my chest, as if something is trying to keep me on Earth. This realm is so dark and miserable. I prefer Earth, I think. I can't remember why I thought coming here would help. It's always the same: empty and dark, the air reeking of death, a cold abyss that never changes. Earth is different—alive, full of color. What's going on with me? I feel this ache, like I've forgotten something important. I should get back to the list. The obligation is rising again, weighing on me for delaying. The next one is in Scotland.

"Scotland," I repeat, a tiny flicker of excitement in my voice, as if the place connects me to something.

A memory, maybe? I depart from the Void to reach the next name, and as I enter the living realm, I feel it again—déjà vu. The sensation is strange, since I remember nothing before that last woman. I don't eat, I don't sleep, and I don't feel—not like humans do. I simply am. I have a job to do, and the never-ending list demands I keep moving or everything will fall apart. I wonder what I look like. There are no mirrors in the Void, and I'm not human, so I must appear terrifying to them.

But then, a memory flashes—a woman looking at me through a reflection in water. It's me. I was the woman. More glimpses crowd my mind, stirring up more questions than answers. Something is buried deep inside me, something I should remember—but it won't come.

"Back to work," I mutter as I step into the mortal realm.

The house appears before me—small, wooden, nestled in soft green grass and tall trees. Its bright red front door seems to welcome me, and a chill creeps up my spine. I don't know why I chose to appear outside. Do I do this often? Or is this part of the change?

Inside, the woman I've come for sits in a wooden rocking chair by a dying fire, the only light in the house. Her long white hair hides half her face, and she cradles a photo album atop a quilt in her lap. One photo in particular pulls at me. My eyes land on a black-and-white image of a little girl holding a teddy bear, standing in front of this very house. She feels familiar. How? I must've reaped her. Once I take a life, I forget—I have to forget—so I can keep doing the job. So why am I remembering?

I know I'm here to collect this woman, she's on her last life but this tug in my chest keeps intensifying, like I'm on the edge of remembering something crucial. She hasn't even looked up at me. Just keeps flipping through the album. How odd. I glance at a mirror on the wall and see myself—this time, a man with tan skin. I must take human forms to comfort them. That makes sense. That has to be it. I need to get back to reaping. I need to push away these feelings.

"How can you turn the pages in my presence?" I ask, and immediately regret it.

The words slip out before I can stop them. I pause, expecting the entire realm to explode—or for the ring to consume me in fire and turn me to dust—but nothing happens. At least, not what I expected.

"Because, Great Grandpa, I am your kin. Of course, I can move as you do," the woman says with a soft, familiar tone and smiles at me, as if she truly believes I'm her kin.

Suddenly, my mind floods with memories, so many, I can't focus. I quickly become overwhelmed. The floodgates are open, and all I can do is let them fill the emptiness within me. My eyes fix on the album, on a picture of a man holding hands with the most beautiful woman I've ever seen, and a small girl between them, sharing their smile.

"Great Grandpa Jameson, you don't seem yourself today. Are you okay?" She asks me like I'm the one holding the album, not the ring.

"Who is that?" I ask, pointing to the photo.

"Do you remember?" she says, then turns the page to a portrait of the same man in a British Royal Marine uniform—one I instantly recognize.

"This was your family. I'm all that's left," she says, letting a tear roll down her cheek.

"I was Jameson Case," I say, no longer caring to guard my words.

I built this house. I lived here with my wife and daughter, but it feels so long ago. She turns another page. My eyes lock on the date, 1802. I see my father and brothers helping me raise the framing of this very home. I remember walking these halls, visiting the only pub in Kirkcaldy, Scotland. She called me Great Grandpa. Could she really be my descendant?

I was human!

Just moments ago, I would've sworn all I've ever known was auditing lives and keeping the dead. Now, with each returning memory, I feel like I'm reclaiming the truth—and it's intoxicating. I had a life. A family. But how did I go from Jameson Case to a soulless husk bound to the Void? I feel it pulling me, trying to wake me from this dream. It must be a dream.

"Are you ready?" I ask her, trying to sound emotionless, to follow protocol.

"I've been waiting for you what feels like forever, Great Grandpa," she says with such love that I nearly lose my composure.

"Do you remember me?" I ask, desperate now.

"Of course I do. We've met before. You always appear differently, but I know it's always you. We never forgot you. Every year, on her death day, we shared your story—your sacrifice. We made sure your legacy lived on," she says, turning another page.

I'm frozen. I can't remember the great deed she speaks of, but perhaps it's tied to this tireless role I now serve, maintaining the balance between life and death. The Void tugs at me harder now. I must finish my task.

"I don't know who you think I am," I insist. "But you're mistaken." I have to say it.

It's too much. These memories, this flood of emotion, I can't bear it. She just smiles knowingly, looks down at the album in her lap, and taps a page. Then, she lifts it, showing me, a worn letter nestled inside. A warm peace washes over me as I read.

To the love of my life Beth and our beautiful daughter Ray. I pray this letter finds you well.

Please know that I love you both more than I can ever express in these words. What I do now, I do so that you may both live. I know it may hurt you, but I promise we will reunite one day—and on that day, we will be free. I gladly give my life for you both, and I want you to live knowing I'm always watching over you. You are the light of my life, and I could not live in a world without you, so this is the only way forward. Trust in me and I will find you again.

Forever yours,

Jameson Case

Eternally your loving husband and father.

...

Each word is an assault on the hollow shell I've become. My heart stirs, beating as though life has returned to me. A tingling sensation starts in my head and runs down to my toes. Before I can process any of it, I vanish from the home. The other realm pulls me back, uncaring of my wants or thoughts.

Did I write that letter? Was I really a husband and father? I was once alive. I had a family. The list presses into my consciousness, reminding me I failed to reap the woman in Scotland. There will be consequences. I can't remember everything, but I see glimpses—brown hair, a little girl laughing, the red door of that house. That was my home. I loved them, and they loved me.

"AHH!" I scream in frustration into the great empty Void but only my own voice echoes back.

No soul here to watch me unravel. I try to throw the ring, but I can't. It's part of me—I of it. Have I been doing this since the 1800s? If those memories are real, why am I still here? The list pulls again. The ring obeys. I have work to do. The universe depends on it. What use is it to dwell on a past life I don't fully remember? Maybe it's all a lie.

...

"Are you ready?" I ask immediately, already conflicted—still thinking of my great-granddaughter and the album.

Why does this feel different now? I know what I must do. It's my sacred duty to ensure each soul gets no more than nine lives—never more. That rule is absolute. I stare at the young man before me, Jason Chambers. He's a second from being crushed by a bus or returning to his life, completely unaware of what almost happened. I wonder... does he have a family? My thoughts betray me again. Was I once like him? Am I the harbinger of death or just a man trapped in servitude for something he did two centuries ago?

Jason trembles before me, eyes wide with fear. I glance at the ring. Two lives left. Why won't he just say no? I feel changed. I can't help but remember the home, the woman, the letter. I've never left a soul unaccounted for. Doing so threatens the natural order. But still... I ask again.

"Are you ready?"

"Did I die?" the boy says, a lost look in his eyes, as if he's accepting death.

I decide he will live. I account for one life and send him back, this time, not being hit by the bus. I vanish and continue working through the names on the list.

"Are you ready?" I ask.

"No," a girl named Tracy responds, and back to her life she goes.

"Are you ready?" I ask the next soul on the list.

"No," she answers.

I collect a life and move to the next soul that needs accounting. I work through hundreds of names, trying to distance myself from my cloudy past. It almost works, until—

"Are you ready?" I say aloud, and then realize I remember this young man.

"Jason, why are you back so soon?" I ask.

"I don't want to live anymore. I planned to jump in front of a bus yesterday, but I chickened out I guess, so today I took a bottle of pain pills I found in the cupboard." Jason replies.

"I am ready," he says.

"You willingly took your own life? Very well," I respond, and take his life. I escort him to the next realm.

I didn't change anything by making the decision for him. He jumped in front of the bus, and I gave him another chance—but he still died. Fate is always one step ahead. I don't like how this is making me feel. My chest aches with a dull pain, as if I had a heart. I need to get back to work. I find myself back in Scotland. I recognize the house as mine. I let out a deep breath and step inside once again. It feels like the ring is pushing me to fix my mistake, as if it has a mind of its own.

"Hello?"

She answers, "Welcome back. I am ready now, Great Grandpa—if you are?"

"I cannot take you yet. I have so many unanswered questions," I say, honesty and desperation in my voice.

"Do you know what happened to my family after I left?" I ask, staring into her eyes.

She smiles for a moment. Then her eyes fill with tears as she looks up at me. Her large emerald eyes stir memories—luscious green hills, a child's laughter. She is of my blood. She *has* to be real.

"I know that you sacrificed yourself to save my great-grandmother, your daughter, and her mother from death over two hundred years ago. They were sick with plague and down to their last beads, so you used your gift to save them."

As she speaks the words, my chest tightens. A ringing grows in my ears.

"If that is true then what became of my family?" I ask, begging for more answers, not knowing how deeply they'll cut.

"The Case family lived in this home you built for the last two hundred years. Even after you left, we remained and we've prospered because of your sacrifice. We made sure your loss was never forgotten. Now I am the end of our story in this home, I fear—I was not blessed with a bairn."

So, they lived full lives. But without me. Sadness fills my chest. Something dangerous stirs in my mind. Rage, anger, and resentment swirl inside me—new, foreign feelings I don't know how to control. She is the last of my line and I missed all of it. I've been cursed to collect souls for all these years, to ferry the dead, while others lived and loved. I was able to save them but why, then, is my debt not yet paid? The thought cools my anger and replaces my madness with pride. I was remembered as a hero.

"Are you ready, my child?" I ask, hoping to end this before I do something I'll regret.

Going down this path won't help me. I can't undo the past. At least, I don't think I can. If I made that sacrifice back then, I must have understood the cost. I must have been willing to pay it.

"For you, I have always been ready, Great Grandpa. Let us take our leave of this place together," she says, standing. I hold out the ring and collect her last bead.

"Then leave we shall," I say, and take her soul to the next realm, so that she may know peace.

For a moment the thought crosses my mind to attempt to cross with her, but then a force pushes me back as a flash of light leaves me alone again. I feel different now. Awake. Like I've been lost for two hundred years and suddenly, I'm in control again. I'm not sure if that's good or bad, but I do know this; I prefer it to the husk I was.

"I am Jameson Case," I say aloud as I finally find my identity.

I glance at my reflection in a nearby lake, one the ring brought us to after delivering my kin. It still feels like a dream, but it must be real. One thing I know for certain, I will do things differently from now on. I am alone in this after all. I can't stop the growing hunger in my chest as I see Jameson—the man I once was—staring back at me. I *want*, for the first time in forever. I want my wife's love again. My daughter's laughter. I want to live.

"I will…"

CHAPTER 7
CIAN: THE DATE

I'm still in disbelief that we're going out on a date tonight. I can't stop thinking about that kiss. I'm not sure what came over me. It was like I wasn't thinking for once and just let myself feel. I really wanted to kiss her so I did and her lips were so soft, and each kiss was intoxicating—so much so, I couldn't stop... until she stopped me. I'm craving more just thinking about her, but I know she was pretty mad that I surprised her like that. She didn't stop me for what felt like an hour though, which would imply she liked it, at least a bit.

Next time I kiss her, I'll ask for permission first. Just to be sure. What am I saying? I've never had to ask for a kiss before. Girls love to kiss me. And I know she enjoyed it just as much from how she kissed me back, from the way her hips pressed into mine. But she's different. I can't figure her out, and it's driving me crazy. I can't stop thinking about her. I want more. I close my eyes and picture those green eyes staring into mine, as if we're the only two people in the world.

My breath deepens, my pulse quickens as I picture her sexy curves and that flowing red hair. She gets to me without even trying—our attraction is effortless. I change outfits three times before settling on my favorite dark blue jeans and a black shirt that lets my arms shine. I really want her to see that I'm not the guy I used to be or the guy I pretended to be a year ago when we collided. Still way too early for the date, I decide to swing by her work and support Vale on her big day.

Vale texted me the other day that she got her big break and asked if I'd come support her and at least pretend to be interested in one of her paintings. Of course, I came for Vale. Seeing Inara again is a bonus. The art gallery is packed when I walk in. A woman, who I assume must be their boss Peggy, greets me with a suspicious look. She clearly doesn't know who I am, and by her expression, probably thinks I don't belong. I've been asked to leave more than one art gallery before just because of how I look.

"Excuse me, sir. This is an invite-only opening," she says, gesturing back toward the exit.

"I'm on the list," I say, walking past her.

She doesn't dare try to stop me.

"Who would invite him to my gallery?" Peggy mutters, not even bothering to keep it quiet.

It takes all my willpower not to respond. Instead, I scan the room for Vale.

"Cian?" Inara says, surprised, and quickly walks over to me which immediately makes Peggy back off.

"Hi. I wanted to come support Vale on her big day. Congratulations, Vale, by the way," I say, giving her a half wave.

She's busy talking to a possible buyer about twenty feet away but manages a small smile my way.

"That's really sweet of you," Inara says, tightening her grip on my hand.

"It's the least I could do. She rarely asks for help and has been there for me more times than I care to admit." I pause.

"You look gorgeous, by the way, sweetheart." I kiss the hand that's still holding mine.

"Thank you… and of course, please look around. Peggy said if we don't sell anything, we're both out of jobs." Inara blushes and laughs, trying to play it off like a joke.

"Wow. She has way more paintings than I thought. These are all… what she remembers from her deaths?" I whisper.

"Yeah. Vale is something else. You haven't even seen them all," Inara says, waving toward the massive wall covered in Vale's dark, ominous paintings.

Inara gives me a tour of the gallery, showing me all of Vale's work while we wait for her to finish with the potential customer.

"So? Did that guy buy one of your paintings? You were talking to him for at least thirty minutes," Inara asks as Vale approaches.

"No," Vale sighs.

"He said they were too dark for him and went on about how the brush strokes were, too deep and broody for his energy." She rolls her eyes.

"Then he tried to get my number."

She looks at me.

"Cian, thank you for coming, but you might as well go home. No one's going to buy any of my work. I'm sorry, Inara." Vale lowers her head in defeat.

I leave them and walk back into the lobby of the gallery with purpose. One painting catches my eye. I pause, drawn to it. I don't recall Vale ever telling me about dying in a car crash with a semi-truck. I scan the paintings slowly as I make my way back, then stop in front of the one that called to me. A chill runs down my spine. A familiar rush. Vale is full of surprises.

"I'll take this one," I say loud enough for the entire gallery to hear.

"I just finished that one this week… it's my favorite," Vale replies.

"You don't have to buy it, Cian. I'm pretty sure Peggy won't fire us. Even if she would, it's not something you have to fix."

But this painting does something to me. Normally, I don't care much for art. But the way she painted the shadows wrapping around the man, and those streaks of blue, red, and green. It's beautiful. I feel tied to it, like I'm looking at a version of myself. The man is clearly hurting. Alone. Surrounded by chaos.

"I don't recognize him… but his blue eyes are haunting."

"You don't really want to buy this, do you?" Vale asks, nervously laughing.

This one is so dark and brutal, but those small swirls of blue, green, and red—they bring hope. The painting stirs something deep inside me, emotions I thought were locked away forever. I suddenly can't move. I just stare into the painting—for what feels like eons.

"Cian, are you okay?" Inara asks, her hand gently touching my arm.

I shake off the trance. "Yes, of course. I want to buy this painting. Do you take card?"

"You really don't have to buy it," Vale says quickly.

Out of nowhere, Peggy swoops in and snatches my card before either of them can stop her.

"This one's four thousand. I'll go ring it up for you," she says, already halfway to the register.

"Perfect. Now I just need to figure out where to hang it," I say, suddenly remembering my tiny apartment barely has a wall big enough to display this masterpiece, which is easily larger than my TV.

I chuckle and turn back to the painting. I need this. Inara is still in shock, frozen mid-expression through the entire exchange. I sign the receipt, and Peggy snaps her fingers, gesturing for Vale and Inara to wrap the purchase.

"I'll see you tonight, sweetheart," I say, leaving with my new treasure.

"Okay," Inara replies softly, still stunned—probably because I just dropped four grand on a painting Vale would've given me for free.

"Thank you!" Vale calls out, running after me and hugging me tight like a python squeezing my ribs.

"You don't have to thank me. Your art is amazing. It's worth every penny," I say, heading out.

"Cian, wait!" Inara calls, chasing after me.

I turn just in time, almost colliding with her. She leans in and plants a soft kiss on my cheek before dashing back into the gallery. No words. Just that. My cheeks flush red, and I'm grinning the entire way home. I unwrap the painting as soon as I walk in. I need to see it one more time before getting changed for our date—can't wear the same thing twice. She always wears something new, and I want to match her energy.

I settle on my favorite blue shirt and head out to pick her up. On the way, all I can think about is that kiss. It wasn't even on the lips, but the way it made me feel... like I was back in high school again. This girl is dangerous. Buzz. I press the obnoxious apartment buzzer. I try to wait patiently, but someone's coming out, so I slip in. I am thirty minutes early so she's probably still getting ready. In the Marines, being on time meant being late, and that's a hard habit to break.

"Special delivery," I say, knocking on her teal-colored door, my eyes catching the silver number five that looks like it's ready to fall off.

She opens the door, expecting a package.

"Sorry about the wait. You can put the package in here," she says casually and looks up.

"Oh! Cian you're early."

"Wow." That's all I can say.

My jaw drops, and I don't even make a crude joke about the "package." Her red hair is a halo around her face, and that short green dress hugs her in all the right ways. Her black heels pull it all together, accentuating every curve. I've never been jealous of a dress before. I just stand there, door open, drinking her in like a work of art.

"Are you okay?" she asks, a small smile playing on her lips but I see panic behind her eyes.

"You look absolutely beautiful," I finally say, still in awe.

"Wait... is that what you're wearing out?" she asks, turning to head back into her apartment.

"I knew it. He doesn't care about this date. I'm such an idiot," she mutters.

"Hold it!" I step inside, only to be met by her four-legged bodyguard.

"Spencer, stop. It's okay, boy. This is just Cian and he'll be leaving now," she says, voice sharp.

"Please, just give me a second to explain. I swear I'm taking this date as seriously as a heart attack. I should've told you where we're going, I get that now. I've got a change of clothes in the car that'll match you better."

"I'll just change. Give me a—" Inara says before I cut in.

"Don't you dare. You look stunning, and it would be a crime not to show you off in that dress."

I reach for her hand and give her a gentle spin, dipping her at the end, our faces inches apart. She blushes, smiling as her hair catches the light, glowing like fire. Her green eyes lock onto mine, and the world narrows to just us. For a second, I forget the date, the reservations, everything. I twirl her back into my arms and sneak a kiss on her cheek.

"Spencer, down boy," she says, laughing.

"Sorry, he gets a little jealous when I dance with anyone else. He's been the only man in my life this past year and we often have dance parties."

She grabs his front paws and spins around the apartment like a fairy tale. Then she lets him down, and he trots over to greet me. I scratch behind his ear and find the spot—his leg goes wild.

"He's a cool pup," I say, standing as Inara steps close.

"Wow. He likes you. He usually hates men. Tried to bite the last guy he met."

"Not surprising. Animals love me," I grin and wink.

She smirks in response.

"So... where are you taking me tonight?"

"It's a surprise," I say, giving Spencer one last pet.

"Okay, well, I guess I'm ready," she says.

"I don't think we can leave just yet," I say, pulling a small teal box from my pocket.

"I saw this the other day and thought of you." I hand it to Inara, and her face lights up.

That smile? Worth every penny.

"Cian?" It's the only word she manages as her fingers wrap around the box.

She fumbles with the ribbon, her hands nervous. After a moment, I pull out my knife and cut it for her, like any gentleman would. For a split second, her face flashes with surprise, maybe even a little fear, but it fades as she remembers what she's holding. Her smile returns.

"There. Now you can open it," I say, slipping the knife back into my pocket.

"Do you always carry a knife?"

"Yes. Since the Marines. You can never be too careful. Plus, I use this thing almost every day—opening something… stabbing something…" I grin, hoping the joke lands.

She laughs and turns her attention back to the box. I watch her carefully, hoping she likes it. The moment I saw it in that window; I pictured it around her neck. And after this past year… let's just say she deserves something special.

"Oh my… Cian, it's beautiful. But I can't accept this." She tries to hand it back.

"I saw it and knew it belonged on you. It's nonrefundable, sweetheart. Now turn around."

I take the necklace from the box and motion for her to spin with a flick of my hand. She does, brushing her hair aside. I unclasp the chain and gently place it around her neck, and become distracted while I fasten it. I have to stop myself from kissing the soft skin just beneath her ear.

"I've always wanted one of these. It's a bean—just like the one in Millennium Park," she says, fingertips grazing the silver charm.

"I love the Bean. Lost count of how many times I've been. I hoped you'd feel the same."

She turns, throws her arms around me, and kisses me—quick, but it sends a jolt through my chest.

"Thank you, Cian."

That reaction? I'd buy her the world if it meant getting that again.

"I think we can leave now. Bye, Spencer. Be a good boy," she says, planting a kiss on her pup's snout.

Out at the car, I hold the passenger door open for her. Her hair brushes my face as she passes, her perfume wrapping around me like a warm haze.

"Is this new?" she asks, peeking inside.

"Yeah. Just got it. Midnight black BMW M5. Leather seats. You like it?"

"Like it? I love this car! I knew you had money—buying Vale's painting didn't even phase you, but I didn't realize you could afford something like this."

"I do alright," I say, grinning.

"But I don't broadcast it. People tend to act different when they find out I don't have to work. Besides, money's not everything."

"Ready to go, sweetheart?" I ask, still holding her door.

Months ago, I overheard her telling Vale this car was her dream. I'm not a car guy, but I appreciate well-crafted things. And since I've got the money… why not make tonight unforgettable? Maybe it helps make up for a year of tension and misfires.

"Can I drive?" she asks, grinning like a kid who just got away with something.

"As you wish, sweetheart." I shut the passenger door and circle around to open the driver's side.

"Over 600 horsepower under the hood? Yes, please." She adjusts her seat, scrolling through radio stations like she's been here a thousand times.

I try to act cool while mentally mapping a route to Piece Pizza in Wicker Park, without ruining the surprise. She tests the limits of the car, and somehow, we get there in one piece—and in record time. The line stretches out the door, but my friend Jackie hooked me up with a table in the back.

"Ever been here?" I ask as we pass by the hungry and clearly jealous crowd.

"No, not really a pizza girl. Is this a brewery too?"

"Yeah. Great food, great beer. I come mostly for the pizza." I rest my hand on the small of her back as she walks in front of me.

The place is packed. The music's barely audible over the crowd. I pull out her chair, and we sit at a small oak table with a hunting lodge vibe. Cozy. Close. Perfect. The waiter appears quickly—perks of being a regular.

"Evening, Jackie. We'll take the small BBQ chicken, mashed potato, and goat cheese pizza. And a small pepperoni, pineapple, and jalapeños. Two drafts of Zombie Dust," I say, confident and ready.

Inara raises an eyebrow, her face a mix of confusion and slight frustration.

"Do you trust me?" I ask, reaching for her hand. It's delicate, slightly cold in mine.

She hesitates… but nods. I make a mental note, next time let her choose.

"So, you come here a lot?" she asks.

"Love this place. Not far from my aunt's old place in Lincoln Park. We used to—"

I stop. Look away. The words sting more than I expect. Just like that, I'm back there. The memory blindsides me. The night I betrayed her. The guilt. The silence. I never got the chance to make it right. She died thinking I didn't care. I'd give anything to tell her how wrong she was. Inara squeezes my hand, and I'm surprised by how hard it is not to pull away. Her touch is comforting in a way I haven't felt since Aunt Clare. I don't let people in, not since the funeral. Not since I sat there alone, just me and a late lawyer.

"Did your aunt pass when you were young?" she asks gently.

"You never talk about your family."

"She died just after my tenth birthday… just after a fight she had with my parents. A fight I caused." I swallow the lump in my throat, blinking back the tears I've trained myself to never show.

Her eyes don't waver. She's not looking for drama. She's offering care. Real care. That smile… it's like a lifeline.

"I'm so sorry. I can't imagine how hard that must've been," she says softly, rubbing the top of my hand with her fingertips.

She leans in even closer, something I didn't think was possible in this tight space. I'm filled with something warm and unfamiliar. I've never let anyone in this far. And honestly, it scares the hell out of me. Inara is dangerous in the best way. This isn't just attraction anymore. It's something real.

Thankfully, the pizza arrives. Perfect timing.

"Yes. Pizza time," I say, plating slices for both of us.

I offer her peppers and parmesan before dousing my own in both, red and white, like Christmas.

"You're gonna love it," I say, smiling.

"I can't believe it took us this long to do this. I'm really glad you asked me out, Cian." Her head tilts slightly, and I'm stunned into silence.

Is this date actually going well? I nod, afraid I'll ruin it by speaking, and we both take a bite. Melty cheese, creamy mashed potatoes, smoky BBQ sauce—it's as good as ever.

"Hmm... this is actually good. I was scared for a minute. The toppings sounded weird, but honestly? Best pizza I've ever had," she says between bites, finishing a slice faster than even me.

As she says the words, I grin and confidently exclaim, "I knew you would!"

We polish off nearly all of the pizzas and a couple rounds of Zombie Dust before Inara's ready for the next part of our date. We stroll down the block to one of my favorite spots—Jeni's Ice Cream—for dessert.

"I'll let you order for yourself this time," I say as we reach the counter, "but you really can't go wrong with the cream puff."

"Good, because I'm more than capable of making up my own mind," Inara replies, a little sass in her voice as she playfully presses her hand against my chest before stepping forward to order.

"So, whatever happened to your aunt's old place? You mentioned it was nearby," she asks, sampling her third flavor like she's judging a national competition.

Her question catches me off guard. No one's talked to me about Aunt Clare since the funeral. I haven't been back to her house since I left for the Marines, except for the time someone broke in and the occasional maintenance check. I always plan to return, but somehow, I never do. Silence lingers until Inara asks for yet another sample. I place a hand gently on her shoulder, and when she turns to face me, I meet her eyes.

"Would you like to see it?" I ask, nodding toward the eight sample spoons still in her hand.

"We can go after you, you know... decide."

"I'll take the butter cake," she says softly, almost shyly.

"But honestly, they're all so good. Thank you."

That voice. That moment. It gives me pause. Should I really be doing this? I'm not exactly stable. And with this curse... I could die tomorrow saving a bus full of kids or something equally absurd. The idea plays like a reel in my head every day; dying heroically to make sense of it all. My spiraling is interrupted by the sight of Inara chomping down on her ice cream cone like an alligator on prey.

"I'm ready," she says, flashing a devious smile.

"Okay, I guess we're really doing this. Her house is a block or two from the zoo, just a couple miles from here. Want to drive or walk?"

"A walk sounds perfect. It's beautiful out tonight." She leans in and steals a bite of my cream puff.

I let her. We head outside, conversation light and easy, the kind of talk that makes you forget time. But beneath the surface, my nerves are building. Going back to Aunt Clare's house feels like opening a wound that never healed. It was her home first, and even though she left it to me, I've never called it mine.

"Let's play twenty questions," Inara says, her voice light and excited.

"I'm game. I'll go first… what's your favorite song?" I ask.

"Impossible question. I could never choose and it depends entirely on my mood," she says with absolute conviction. I take a mental note in the hopes that this valuable information will serve me well later.

…

An hour later, we're nearly there. Just a few more feet, and I'll be home. But when we reach the gate, I stop. My feet won't move.

"Are we here?" she asks gently.

"I can't do this," I whisper.

"This was a mistake."

I pull away, turning so my back is to the house, heart pounding in my ears. It's all coming back to me. My failures and my shame.

"We don't have to go in, Cian," she says, stepping closer.

"But I'm here with you, no matter what you decide."

Her words hit harder than I expect. They mean something. And I can't remember the last time someone stood by me like this. I dig deep and remember I'm a Marine. I can do this. I will not be afraid of the past any longer. Let dead things stay dead.

"Let's go," I say, gripping her hand tightly as we approach the door.

Aunt Clare's house looks almost exactly the same, aside from needing a fresh coat of paint. It's like stepping back in time. The memories hit fast, one after the other. For a split second, it feels like she's still inside, waiting for me. I wish I could introduce her to Inara. She would've adored her. My hand hovers over the doorknob, frozen in place. But this time, I'm not alone. Inara's here, and I'm holding her hand.

"I'm ready," I say, and I step through the door with her close behind.

The stale air rushes out to greet me, carrying the scent of dust, old wood, and something uniquely... Aunt Clare.

"Hello? If anyone's squatting in here, get out now!" I shout as I flick on the lights.

Inara gives me a puzzled look but grabs my hand when we both hear a sound. A small gray mouse darts across the floor and vanishes under a door.

"You haven't been here in a while, huh?" she teases, and we both burst out laughing.

"Not in years," I admit.

"She left me the house, but I could never call it home. The grief always came rushing back too fast. I've carried the key with me ever since; I've just never had the guts to come back. Until now."

"Thank you," I say, turning to her.

"If it weren't for you, I still wouldn't have come home." I kiss her cheek gently.

This house... it was more my home than anywhere I've lived since. Before my parents' accident, we bounced around, renting and moving every year. I had more addresses by sixteen than most people have in a lifetime. Looking around now, I feel something I haven't in years. A warm ache in my chest. It lingers, just long enough to remind me I'm alive. Then I push it back down.

"Aunt Clare understood me in a way no one else ever had... and I thought no one ever would again." I blink.

"Oops. Did I just say that out loud?"

I pivot, trying to lighten the mood. "Want a tour?"

"Yes! I love seeing different floorplans!" she squeals, bouncing a little as she looks around the entryway, forgetting my slip completely.

Thank God she lets that window stay shut. I'm barely holding it together, and I don't want to break down on our first date. I start with the grand staircase, then the kitchen which, frankly, could use a remodel.

"The house is gorgeous," Inara says.

"Your aunt had impeccable taste. For being empty all these years, I'm impressed. I really thought it'd be condemned… or at least haunted."

I laugh. "I pay the neighbor to handle the upkeep. But haunted by Aunt Clare and Uncle Jay? Honestly, I wouldn't mind."

…

After the tour, we settle onto the old living room couch. Her things are still here, untouched. The house is still a home, just one layered in dust, cobwebs, and the occasional mouse who probably considers us the trespassers now. I check my watch.

"Damn, we won't make it now," I say, standing to my feet.

"Won't make it where?" she asks.

"I planned to take you to the zoo and end our date by the lake, but they'll be closed by now," I say, disappointment creeping into my voice.

I feel like I've failed her by not making this date as special as she is.

"Cian, this date has already been amazing. Maybe our next date can be at the zoo," Inara says, rising to join me.

"I'm in no hurry to head home. I already asked Vale to check in on Spencer for me tonight," she adds, placing her hand gently on my chest.

Her hand is light, but the weight of it makes it hard to breathe. I'm continuously surprised by this woman. Without thinking, I move to the corner near the window and pry up a loose floorboard.

"I want to show you something," I say as I pull the boards away.

"Aunt Clare and I had this secret spot in the floor where we used to hide treasures and secret messages. We found it by accident…one day I tripped while playing with her dog Shelby, and she pulled up the loose board, ready to fix it herself. Instead, we discovered this little space. Just a few feet wide and deep, but perfect for hiding anything we didn't want found."

With the board removed, I freeze. Suddenly, I'm nine again, hoping Aunt Clare left me something—maybe an action figure or one of her secret letters I had to decode with the codex she made for me. They always ended with "I love you" and some reminder to eat my vegetables. But they felt like magic.

"What's that?" Inara asks, stepping closer.

"She left me something," I whisper. The hairs on my arms rise as a wave of emotion surges in my chest. Only Aunt Clare and I knew about this spot.

She must've known I'd come back one day. I lift out a dusty old box and slowly open the lid. Regret hits me like a brick. I could've opened this years ago.

"Open it! The anticipation is killing me," Inara says, practically climbing into my lap.

"I... I don't believe it," I mutter, staring into the box.

Inside is Aunt Clare's journal, a few folded documents, and an old watch—its hands frozen in time, probably before I was even born. My chest aches. She still cared, even after everything I did. Guilt and relief war inside me, until Inara joins me on the floor, her eyes shining with tears as she looks at the box.

"She knew she'd never see me again," I say softly.

"This was her way of saying goodbye."

"This is so beautiful," Inara whispers.

"She left you a journal...and is that a Ranger action figure?" Her eyes water, and I know mine do too.

"She still cared about me, even after I—"

"Of course she did," Inara interrupts gently.

"She clearly loved you. She left you this and this amazing house. I never met her, but she must've adored you, Cian. Why would you think she didn't?"

I'm not ready to unpack that yet. But I want to talk to her. I want her to know the real me. It's terrifying… but this whole day has been full of firsts.

"I betrayed her trust," I finally say.

"And she died before I could apologize. I thought… I thought she would've stopped loving me. But seeing this, I know she didn't. I was wrong."

"Oh, Cian." Inara says, rubbing my back in slow, soothing circles.

"I'm so glad you're finally opening up. I'm sorry she's not still here."

"What does the note say?" she asks, pointing to the taped message on the journal's cover.

I peel the tape back slowly and read the note aloud,

My Dear Cian,

I knew you would find this journal. I want you to know that I love you so much. I'm sorry I won't be there to see you grow into your power and become the man I know I'll be proud of. This journal is everything you'll need to do better than I did. I started writing to cope with the trials of my own childhood, but it became more than that once you were born. I hope it helps you when things feel darkest. Remember, it's not a curse unless you let it be.

P.S. I will love you always and forever. You are the one good thing I leave behind. Watch out for Fate, she hates when we use our power to change the master plan. There are always consequences to our actions and they can sometimes ripple throughout space and time forever. She will step in to stop anyone that threatens this reality. Do not tempt her and remember to always keep your shield up. It will help keep you safe.

Tears fall onto the page, blurring the ink as I reread it again and again. Even now, she finds a way to be here for me. She didn't blame me. She was proud of me. I hold the journal close, as if it could bring her back if I read the words enough times.

"Thank you," I whisper.

I feel lighter. For the first time since I was a kid, I can breathe. She believed in me. And she left me this… not just a goodbye, but a guide.

"Cian, I'm so sorry she's not here with you. What she wrote… may I ask what it said?"

I look into Inara's eyes, glassy with emotion, and I nod.

"Thank you, Inara. You have no idea how much this means to me. I never would've come back here without you. She left me an entire journal full of messages to help me... and because of you, I got a piece of her back."

As we stand, I reach up, cradle her face, and kiss her gently. Her cheeks are flushed, her tears wiped away as we lose ourselves in each other. Time stops. We sink into the couch, tangled together, but I pull back slightly. I don't want this to move too fast. Not yet. We sit in silence for a while. She lays her head on my shoulder, and it's perfect. Her warmth, her scent—vanilla and citrus—it's intoxicating.

She eventually falls asleep, head on my arm. I smile and slowly lay her back on the couch, grabbing a blanket and giving it a good shake—just in case there's an unexpected mouse stowaway. I cover her gently, then return to the hidden compartment and pick up the journal again. I flip through the pages. Each one is filled with Aunt Clare's story and in the margins, newer ink. Notes clearly written for me.

I pause on one page—a large drawing of a gem. A green crystal. It's the only page with color. The text is too faded to read, but there's a map beneath it and a string of numbers. This journal… it's not just memories. It's a puzzle. A message. A path. Inara lets out a soft moan in her sleep, and I smile. I probably should've taken her home but I'm not ready to be here alone. This place will always be Aunt Clare's house to me.

The blanket I covered her with is the same one Aunt Clare used to cover me when I'd fall asleep—on the couch, the stairs, even the bathroom floor once. Grief stirs in me but so does hope. It's confusing. But it's something. A calmness washes over me, gentle and unfamiliar. I don't know the last time I felt this or if I ever have. I look over at Inara, still fast asleep, and smile. I decide we both need rest so I lift her into my arms and carry her upstairs to the bedroom I used to call mine, the only one I can bring myself to walk into right now. I lay her down and slip in beside her, looping my arms around her as I pull the blanket up over us.

Her scent pulls me in, her presence grounding me in the moment. It feels fast but it also feels like I've known her forever. We haven't even slept together yet, which is unusual for me… but Inara is different. And for the first time, I want to let someone see all of me. The heavy weight of my eyelids compels me to join her in sleep, even as a thousand new thoughts race through my mind.

CHAPTER 8
JAMESON: NOT READY

I remember. My beloved family. Everything I sacrificed. I can see their beautiful faces just staring up at me on a cool summer day in the field. I open my eyes and feel a sudden sinking in my chest. I wish I were anywhere but stuck in this damn Void. I want my family back. I want to live again, to feel, to know pleasure, love, even pain. I want those beautiful summer flowers that used to grow in the fields, or the freshly baked pies my wife made for the holidays; the ones I always snuck a bite from before the party started. I can almost smell them when I close my eyes.

But all I'm left with is emptiness. A reminder that this is just a hopeless dream. I'm not mortal anymore. I wonder if there was someone who held this job before me—and if so, how did they escape the curse? Maybe I can find them… and make them take it back. The thought of being free rushes over me like a wave. It becomes the only thought that matters.

If I'm to be mortal again, I need to remember *how* I saved my family… and the deal I made with Death. But the hard truth hits me: I have no idea where to begin. My bloodline has long since passed into the next realm. And I can't even enter that realm. It only accepts those with souls. And that's the crux of my problem. White-hot anger surges through me. Frustration boils. And suddenly—

I'm no longer in the Void. I'm standing in the middle of a cornfield, surrounded by stalks reaching high above me. Why… a cornfield? Did the ring activate on instinct, some desperate reflex to pull me out of that pit? Movement. Something darts through the corn. I don't hesitate—I follow. Nothing escapes me. My presence bends reality; my power closes the distance. I find him. A frightened old man, stumbling and breathless.

"Leave me alone! Just take someone else!" he shouts, trying to flee.

I raise the golden ring, expecting to see I'm here to collect this man's final life. But then I freeze. *Wait...*

"How do you still have so many lives left at your age? And more importantly, how can you move right now?" I step toward him, suspicion rising.

"Just leave! I'm not ready! Take someone else, or—if you have to—take one of mine. Just go!" He pleads, trying to hide from me.

"Who do you think you're talking to?" I snarl.

"Answer my questions—or I'll take all your lives."

"You're not leaving… Why aren't you leaving? It always works when I say that…"

He looks genuinely afraid now.

"Please, don't kill me."

"Do you even know who I am?" I ask, letting him face me fully.

"Yes! But... I'm not ready. Please, I beg you. Take anyone else, just not me."

"Why do you keep saying that? Take someone else? That's not how this works," I growl, frustrated.

Senile old fool.

"You don't know?" he whispers, as if discovering something terrifying.

"I'm not the one who owes answers," I snap.

"And I'm out of patience."

"I'm sorry!" he says, panicking.

"It's just—I don't know why. But ever since I was a boy, whenever you came for me, I could move. I'd beg you to take someone else, and... you did. Every time."

That stops me cold. Could it be true? Why hasn't it worked this time? Has something changed... since I got my memory back? I don't know what to do with this information, but a flicker of hope stirs in me. Could this be used to save myself?

"I've done it dozens of times over the years," he continues.

"Your gold… thingy… it glows red, and then you leave. I just figured you took someone else who still had all nine lives."

I look at the ring. It hasn't changed. But I step toward him, intrigued. Does he have my old power? He can deny death. But not this time. Maybe even this power has limits. I know I should reap him. He's outlived his destiny. But something in me hesitates. Maybe… he can help me.

"I'll make you a deal," I say.

"Help me solve my problem, and I'll let you live."

"Anything! What do you need?"

"It's simple," I say.

"I need to become mortal again. How do I do that?"

The Void tugs at me. It's already pulling me back.

"Whoa. I—I have no clue how to help with that. That's way above me. I just assumed you were Death. Like, an angel or a reaper or something. I didn't know you were once human."

His eyes go wide with fear as he stumbles backward.

"You're scared. Good. You should be," I say coldly.

"I hold your life in my hand. And you've failed me."

I have an idea. It could end me. But if I'm right…

"Wait!" he cries.

"Maybe this will help! I'm not the only one who can do this! Years ago—I met a woman. She was… terrifying. Way more powerful than me. She had this old leather-bound journal and these chilling blue eyes. Said she was older than she looked."

Now he has my attention.

"What's her name?" I ask, halting my plan.

"Something with a C. Or maybe a K? Carol? Karen? I don't know! I don't remember!" he says, voice frantic.

"You're lying," I growl.

"Trying to escape fate. But you should know—your time is now."

I raise the ring. His lifeline glows. Four beads remain. This is new to me—off script. I don't even know if this will work. But before I second guess myself, I reach out. I pluck a bead. It glows red and dissolves into ash in my fingers. Another—same result. Only two remain.

"Please—!"

Before he can finish, I remove the last two. He drops. Dead. The Void grabs me. I don't even have time to ferry his soul.

"Rats!" I mutter in the darkness.

"Well... that didn't work."

Still, something feels... different. He'll follow me soon. Lost souls always do, drawn to me until I deliver them to rest. But I feel something strange in my chest. Something new. Maybe taking his life was wrong. But maybe it was also a step in the right direction. I've been dead a long time. Maybe I just need enough stolen lives to come back. It gives me hope I am close to living again.

Suddenly, an overwhelming pull takes over. I'm certain now that there must be a way for me to live, and those mortals the old man spoke of must be the key. They have some special ability, and I'll use that to break free of this prison. I crave life so badly that nothing will stop me—no cost is too high for the chance to see my family again. I'll use the list to guide me to the next soul, and I'll take their lives for my own. This time, it will work.

"Next up, Inara James. Chicago, Illinois. See you soon, my dear," I whisper into the empty Void, where only I and the tormented soul of that old man can hear.

"Don't worry, old man. Once I regain my life, I won't forget you. I'll make sure you reach the next realm," I say to him as I step into the mortal realm.

I didn't mean to leave him behind, but I can't risk bringing anyone else along now that I'm breaking every rule. Surely something exists to stop me. Still, I am resolute—I'll live again at any cost. No more wasting time on anyone else. My plan is simple: take one life for myself, try to add it to my lifeline, and repeat until it works. If I find another special mortal, I'll force them to help me.

...

I arrive at the house in Chicago and see the girl. She just fell down the stairs and snapped her neck. She's frozen in place. Not special. But she has plenty of lives left to help me make this work. Five attempts. Before I can make my move, someone rushes into the room. He must be another special mortal like the old man—able to move in this suspended moment. I'm furious at first, but then a sliver of joy flickers inside me. What luck to find someone like him so quickly, and he also has five lives to liberate.

He stands by her side like he can stop me. I smile. The thought of him overpowering me is ridiculous. This is going to work—I can practically feel my heart beating again.

"Abacus, she is not ready. I will give you one of my lives in her place," he says before I can strike.

Abacus. I kind of like that name. I let myself get distracted, and before I can act, one of the beads glows green as it transfers to the girl's line, saving her, saving them both. Memories flash. My wife. An object with lifelines and beads. But it's not the golden ring I wear now—it's black, rigid, ancient-looking. Thousands of years old. I see two rows of beads, one glowing green as it slides to the other line...just like with the special mortal. I've seen this before. I am feeling more certain I had this ability when I was alive.

Before I can speak, the Void pulls me back. The transaction is complete. I'm no longer needed in the realm. My plans are ruined. He gave up one of his lives without hesitation. He didn't even know I planned to take all of hers—and his, if he hadn't intervened. I must go back. I'll force him to help me, and I already know exactly how.

"Abacus," I whisper into the Void.

I know this name. But why? Someone must've called me that before. The idea of getting my life back rushes in again. I'm losing sight of the mission. I would have succeeded already if I'd just used my power to stop him from speaking. I am Jameson Case, and I will get my life back. No matter the cost, I will see my family again. I deserve it—after all these years as the gatekeeper, the balance for life and death, blah blah blah.

The list pulls at me, demanding I return to duty. That familiar pressure. I give in and move to the next name. Another one in Chicago. How serendipitous. Michael Jacobson. Four lives left, according to my ring. That won't last. I find myself on a train. He's the conductor. Doesn't matter. I need his beads. I waste no time. In one fluid motion, I pull all four beads into my hand. In less than a second, his lives vanish—and I'm left with ashes. Again.

"Why didn't it work?" I mutter as the Void yanks me back.

Maybe if I find someone with all nine lives, that might be enough. Maybe I need more power at once. The next name: Jennifer Cross. Gary, Indiana. I appear in a hospital room. A young woman lies in a bed, surrounded by machines I don't recognize. The chart reads "coma" and "non-responsive." I lift my ring…only one life left.

"What a waste of my time," I say, sorrow creeping into my voice.

I take the bead. She dies. It turns to dust. The Void pulls me back before I can feel anything. I jump to the next name. I won't stop until I find the one.

"Madam, you don't know me, but thank you for your help in a matter of great importance," I say to the girl with nine lives.

Before I lose my chance, I take them all. This is it. I'm going to live again. But when her beads touch my hand, they vanish like all the others. All nine gone. Nothing to show. What a waste.

"This isn't working," I curse, returning to the Void.

Yet the pull feels weaker. Taking lives must extend my freedom. If I'm going to break this curse, I need more power. I'll keep using the list until I'm mortal again.

...

I've lost count. Beads vanish. Names get crossed off. Now I understand why no one wants to keep their memories for this job. Maybe I erased mine after doing this thousands of times. So many lives taken and I'm still trapped.

"Damn these beads. Why won't you work for me?" I scream into the Void.

It's not so empty anymore, with all the souls I've left behind. I remember the special lad in Chicago. The one who called me Abacus. He might have answers. Maybe he's the key. If only I could teleport to Inara like I do with the list names. I close my eyes, focus—nothing. But I know I've done it before. I was angry, thinking about what I wanted most. I try again. Focus on Inara. Her eyes fixed on him, not me. She knew he'd save her. I open my eyes. I'm in Chicago.

"It worked," I say aloud.

She's in a building filled with art. A museum, maybe. I've never used my power without the list, but I should be able to interact with her, even if she's not dying. Mortals can't see me, though. Time is still moving. This is new. Usually, I enter halfway into their realm, stop time, collect the soul, and return. I imagine a cord tethering me to the Void. It's pulling again. I haven't even reached her yet. My patience wears thin. She's just working in the store. I don't want to tip off the special lad.

He might know things I've forgotten. The Void pulls harder. I give in, return to the list.

"Are you ready?" I ask the next soul.

"I'm not ready to die. Please—"

Too late. I take his lives. Then I fly through the list, taking every bead for myself.

"Maybe you'll be the one," I say to a woman in a red convertible who crashed into a wall in Italy.

Two lives left. I take them both.

"Please," she whispers, just before her beads disappear.

"This isn't working," I growl as I recharge in the Void.

But I keep going. Fueled by bloodlust. I don't know what's happening to me—but I like it. Feelings rush back after each life. My power grows. I love it. Each life I take brings me closer. Eventually, I'll meet the special lad again. He'll tell me his secrets. Thousands of beads, and I'm still chained to the Void. I need more lives at once.

"Gentlemen, I usually do this privately, but I'm experimenting," I say to three men in a wreck outside Michigan.

No survivors.

"Still nothing."

At a pool now. A drowned child. She reminds me of my daughter. The hair, the eyes. Without meaning to, I start taking her last life. How could she be down to her last already? I reach out but stop. I grab the bead and force it back.

"I won't let her die!" I shout.

The bead glows red… then green. It rests on her lifeline. I did it. I saved her.

"Daddy misses you, Ray," I whisper as I'm ripped away.

I used my power to save someone. I'm more powerful than I thought. No more rules. No more list. Am I a monster? Or does one good deed make up for all the rest? Jameson wouldn't have done all this… would he? How did I become this? I think of home. The one Jameson built. The wife with the beautiful hair. The daughter with a kind heart. Suddenly, I'm back in Scotland. Scot pines. Oak trees. The small home. Flashes of memory. My daughter playing. My wife smiling. Wind catching her hair. Her white dress clinging to her figure. I want them back. And just like that, I justify everything. I'm ready to keep going. I only want to live. Be free. Like everyone else.

I deserve it.

CHAPTER 9
INARA: FATE

"Cian?" I whisper, praying Abacus is really gone.

"Are we okay?" I ask, still in shock.

"You're safe now, sweetheart. I won't let anything happen to you. I promise," he says, wrapping his arms tightly around me in a warm embrace.

His voice eases the tension in my body; unclenching muscles I hadn't even realized were tight. I always feel safe with him—and damn, he smells good right now. His eyes, golden and warm, seem to shift in color while you're staring into them. Cian almost makes me forget Abacus was just here. Almost. A shiver climbs up my spine realizing how close I came to losing another life, if not for him. He saved me without hesitation, appearing out of nowhere like some kind of guardian. I'm not used to being protected like that. No one ever has. My last boyfriend ghosted me. The one before that was even worse.

"I had a feeling so I came running to check on you. When I saw Abacus standing there, I couldn't risk you saying yes. I had to act. I'm sorry I made the choice for you," Cian says, pushing me gently to arm's length as his eyes search mine with intensity.

"Cian, you don't have to apologize for saving me. That was... amazing. The most heroic thing anyone's ever done," I say, moving back into his arms.

I'm not ready to let go of him yet. He looks down at me, surprised, and I notice the weight of what just happened pressing on him. He seems wounded, shaken by the encounter. I always saw him as a brute—indestructible, fearless, walking around like he owned the world. But over the last few days, I've seen a completely different side of him. I know I'm falling for him.

"Thank you, Cian. For saving me. But why would I say yes?" I ask, puzzled.

The thought had never crossed my mind.

"I've seen it before," he says quietly, his eyes drifting away.

"I didn't react fast enough to save him."

His arms loosen, and something dark flickers behind his eyes.

"That must've been awful," I say, my voice softening.

"I'm so sorry you went through that. Have you…have you seen a lot of people die?"

"Too many to count. I stopped keeping track when I was a kid. I dropped my shields once, just walking home from school, and saw more than a dozen. It took me a month to pull myself together. I wish I could say that was the only time I slipped up."

He bows his head just enough for me to press a gentle kiss on what I think is his jaw.

"That must've been so hard, especially as a kid. Did you tell your parents?"

"Can we change the subject?" he says gently.

"I don't mean to be rude. I want you to know everything… I just can't go there right now."

Way to go, Inara. You're blowing this. There's no way he'll want another date with the great detective who pokes every wound open. I pivot quickly, desperate to fix things.

"How were you able to move like that when Abacus was here? You were so fast. And then somehow, you got him to use your life instead of mine."

I follow him toward the kitchen, catching the scent of breakfast.

"I know you have a lot of questions, and I'll answer them. All of them, in time. But for now, sit down and I'll finish breakfast. I ran out to grab a few things while you were still sleeping. I hope you like an English breakfast—just like my aunt used to make," he says with a crooked smirk, planting a kiss on my cheek.

"I also picked up fresh orange juice and sliced berries. Just in case," he adds as I settle myself at the kitchen table to watch him work.

"That sounds amazing. And I'm famished. Nearly dying really works up an appetite," I say, trying to lighten the mood and fail based on the somber expression that crosses his face.

"You've been busy," I say, looking around the kitchen filled with platters of food trying to change the topic. Cian is full of surprises.

"What—"

"Again, with the questions," he interrupts, playful now.

"Beautiful, sit back down and relax while I finish cooking. I promise I'll indulge your curiosity afterward, for as long as you'd like."

He touches my shoulder as he moves past me to grab some bread—fresh, of course.

"Toast?" he asks.

"Sure," I say, continuously surprised by this new side of him I am finally getting to experience.

I want to ask more questions, but he's so at ease right now, it feels wrong to break the moment. I can't believe I stayed the night at his place—and that we slept next to each other. Suddenly it hits me that I just nearly lost another life and probably look like a disaster. I haven't showered or brushed my teeth, and I'm in last night's clothes and smeared makeup.

He must think I look like one of those scraggly little creatures from *Fraggle Rock*!

"Coffee, sweetheart?" he says, pulling me out of my spiral.

God, I love when he calls me that.

"Coffee would be great, big guy," I say, immediately blushing as red as the strawberry jam he smeared on my toast.

Big guy? Did I seriously just call him that? I mean… it's a compliment, right? He is a very big guy. And he literally gave up a life for me. Cian pours my coffee and sets down the largest plate of food I've ever seen. So, this is what he meant by English breakfast. I've always wanted to travel overseas. I almost went once in college but let a boy talk me out of it.

"Enjoy," he says, kissing the top of my head, buzzing with energy like we didn't just face off with Death moments ago.

How is he doing this? Cooking, smiling—like nothing happened. He must be a pro at compartmentalizing trauma. I don't know how he's still sane after all he's seen… and yet here he is, making me breakfast.

"Thank you!" I blurt suddenly, startling him mid-sip and nearly causing third-degree burns.

Way to go Inara. Awkward morning, check.

"You never have to thank me for keeping you safe or feeding you, gorgeous. It's my pleasure. And I know we haven't had a chance to discuss this yet but just in case you're getting the wrong impression, let me be clear—This is serious for me Inara. I want you to be mine." His tone is confident, almost arrogant, as he sets down his coffee and steps so close I get chills.

How can this be the same Cian I hated for the last year? All that time wasted, just trying to avoid him, deny that something's clearly been pulling us together. If there was any doubt before, he just crushed it. I swallow the knot in my throat and try to speak.

"Okay," is all I manage to get out as he hovers over me.

"Good. Then it's settled," he says, and then he kisses me, unexpected and powerful, the kind of kiss that makes me ready to agree to whatever he wants.

Pull yourself together, Inara. He is not that hot. Quick, look for flaws—there have to be some. And yet, there he is, drinking his coffee like he's the most perfect man on the planet. He is so incredibly handsome I want to tear off his shirt and li—

"How's the chow?" he asks, cutting off my thoughts, thank God.

"Oh, it's delicious. I don't think I've ever had an English breakfast. I honestly don't know how someone could eat all this food in one sitting. Are these three different kinds of sausage?" I ask, moving the meats around my plate and taking a bite of eggs so I don't seem rude.

"Actually, only one is sausage. The others are white pudding and blood sausage—my favorites," he says, then finishes his plate of food in what feels like a second.

He is dangerous. My brain is sounding every alarm, but for some reason, I don't care. I'm strangely comfortable here with him, like I've known him my whole life. Like he knows the real me, the one I keep hidden. I want to be his. The thought makes me smile. Speaking of him knowing the real me... he has some explaining to do.

"There's clearly a lot you're not telling me, Cian. I want to know everything—just like you promised," I say with a playful tone.

"You're right. I will tell you everything, while you eat." He doesn't argue and gets up to refill his coffee.

He starts with the first time he used his ability to save his aunt, and the little she taught him before she passed. Most of what he knows, though, comes from the lives he lost in the Marines. He talks about his shield, the one that protects him from seeing every death. Without it, all he'd do is watch people die everywhere he goes. Was he shielding when I fell down the stairs?

I never thought about how hard it must've been for him being in the Marines, constantly surrounded by death. He never talks about his service. I recognized one of his medals as a Combat Action Ribbon. My dad had one pinned to his chest at his funeral. It means Cian took a life in combat.

"Without the shield limiting my range, I get pulled into the loss with Abacus every time he shows up to reap someone," he says, rubbing his face with those massive hands.

"I like to think of that place as a limbo between life and death. Because we're not on Earth anymore. There's this dark Void that surrounds you and I have to focus to see where I actually am. Every loss is a bit different though and the time I was pulled into one a few blocks away was so weird, but you don't want to hear about that."

He continues, "I don't know exactly how close someone has to be when they die to drag me in, but I figure it's about a football field—give or take. Even when my parents said Aunt Clare was ill and making up stories, I knew deep down she was right. This is all real."

His gorgeous golden-brown eyes begin to water, and he turns his head away.

"You don't have to do that," I say gently, pulling his jaw so he looks at me.

Cian is opening up to me more than I ever expected, especially for a second date. Can I even call it that? I mean, it's technically the second day of our first date. That counts, right? He also gave a life for me... which feels like something I can never repay. It's a lot to take in.

But I do care about him. He makes me feel like I'm the only woman in the world and that he's all mine. If I'm being honest, I've always had strong feelings for him. And that body? Certainly, doesn't hurt either. I can't be falling for him this fast though. You need to cool it Inara, before you do something you'll regret.

He tells me about a loss on his last deployment. The emotion in his voice brings tears to my eyes, and before I know it, we're curled up on his couch. I'm overwhelmed. He carries so much pain, and here I am, barely out of college, working my dream job at the art gallery with my bestie, thinking life was ruined because I couldn't get those red heels for this date.

"Please don't cry, beautiful. I promise I'm okay. It was years ago, and I have a good handle on this stuff." His hand caresses my face so gently it shocks me that he has that kind of control.

"You've been through so much. Do you regret any of it?" I ask softly.

"Ask me that tomorrow, sweetheart."

"Cian, I... I don't even know what to say."

For the first time ever, I'm speechless.

"I want to clarify something," he says.

"I do have feelings. I just got really good at suppressing them so I could do what had to be done. I had no idea what was happening when I first met Abacus. The second time, it still didn't feel real. I was driving my parents' car. But after seeing him so many times, reading Aunt Clare's journal, and giving away lives... I know, without a doubt, she was right. About everything."

He starts pacing as he gestures around the house.

"You seem so calm and certain all the time," I say.

"I thought you were just an emotionless jerk. But I love that you're opening up to me, showing me the real you. And I really like this side of you—a lot." I reach for his hands.

"Last night, after you fell asleep, I read more of Aunt Clare's journal. I couldn't believe what she went through. She warned me to be careful, not to use my abilities unless absolutely necessary. Her words were full of fear and worry. I never knew there was more to all of this. Her journal... it's incredible." Cian says.

"I never talk about my past," he says.

"It reminds me of everyone Abacus took—my uncle, my parents, my Marines, Aunt Clare... not to mention the hundreds I've watched him reap."

A tear rolls down my cheek, and he catches it with a steady finger.

"I'm so sorry you've had to go through all that. No one should face that alone," I whisper and wrap my arms around him and we hold each other in silence.

Suddenly Cian shifts the mood unexpectedly and begins to dance with me around the room like we've danced together a hundred times.

"I didn't know you could dance," I say, giggling as he suddenly dips me.

Instead of answering, he kisses me. I keep the rest of my questions to myself, for now. That kiss has my head spinning. He twirls me, stopping only when he has me smiling so big my cheeks hurt.

"Let's play Twenty Questions," he says.

"I'll start. What's your favorite kind of music?"

"Well... that's complicated. I have thousands of songs from every genre. Depends on my mood, really."

"Favorite food?" he continues.

"Another hard one. Depends on the day. Sonoran hot dog, pizza, filet mignon, tamales... or maybe a bean and cheese burrito with lettuce, tomato, green sauce, and sour cream."

"You know what? Just tell me what food you hate the most. Music too?" he says, smiling.

He's so much funnier now that I don't see his jokes as digs. He's so handsome its distracting. I can think of a dozen ways we could spend our time right now but this is probably the safer option. If he made a move, I'd let him.

"You're so beautiful," he says, kissing my hand and locking eyes with me.

I glance at my watch.

"Oh no! The time!" I shout.

"I'm going to be late! I have to get to work." I bolt toward the door.

"I'll drive you," he says, catching me before I make it.

"That's sweet, and I had an amazing time but I should get a cab".

Before I can call, he's already on the phone, ordering a rush pickup.

"You don't need to do that," I try to protest.

"It's all set. They'll be here in five minutes," he says, kissing my forehead.

He turns and I frantically begin searching for my purse. I try to pull myself together, but then suddenly he is handing me a bouquet of flowers. He must've hidden them earlier.

"Not as beautiful as you but I hope you like them, Inara. Thank you for giving me the chance to show you the real me and for an unforgettable night." He wraps his muscular arms around me, his chest pressing into mine.

His fingers slide through my hair, tugging gently before he kisses my neck—soft, tender, just enough pressure. Then his lips meet mine. It's the best kiss I've ever had.

Ding dong! The doorbell saves me from myself. His kiss sends heat and electricity through every inch of me. I don't want to stop.

"Your ride is here. We should stop," he says between kisses.

I somehow break free and glance at my watch. If I don't leave now, I'll be late. Peggy once fired someone for being ten minutes late from lunch. I have to go—but his touch...

"I have to go!" I shout and push him back.

Okay, maybe not my most graceful exit. But if I don't leave now, I never will. Before I know it, I'm in the town car he ordered.

"Don't worry, Miss. I have strict orders to get you to work on time. And I'm not about to disappoint that man," the driver says, snapping me out of my Cian-induced fog.

...

"It was amazing, Vale. Cian is nothing like I thought he was," I say, letting out a longing sigh.

"Spill. I want to know everything," Vale says, pulling me toward the back so we can talk in private.

She's literally my best friend and always wants me to share every detail, like we always do, but I'm not sure I'm ready for that. She slams the door shut behind us.

"That's better. Now spill," she says, practically sitting in the same seat as me at our tiny break room table.

"Alright, I confess, it was the most surprising and interesting night of my entire life. He started by taking me to two of his favorite spots around the city. Then took me to this house he inherited from his aunt but refused to live in. We slept together… like not the fun kind, mind out of the gutter. Oh, and Abacus showed up and Cian gave one of his lives for me and then he gave me flowers," I say, trying to downplay just how incredible it all was.

Vale stares at me in shock—definitely because of the Abacus part. I know she wants all the tea, but I'm worried that if I talk about it too much, I'll fall head over heels for him. Vale and I are like sisters. She knows me better than anyone. She can tell I'm holding something back, and I'm pretty sure she knows why, because she just places her hand over mine and smiles.

"Inara, I'm so happy for you both," she says gently.

"He surprised me at every turn. Vale, he was such a gentleman… and he even made me breakfast this morning," I say, still not touching on the most insane part—that he gave up a life for me.

"Let's back up to Cian giving a life for you, and pretend for a second that I even understand how he could do that. You died?" Vale asks, completely distraught as she jumps from her chair to hug me.

"I promise I'm fine. I fell down the stairs and then Abacus was there, but before he could do anything, Cian took charge and forced Abacus to take his bead instead of mine," I say, trying to calm her down.

"It was amazing… and terrifying. I'm still a little in shock, to be honest." I lean back in my chair.

"I didn't know that was you," Vale says, like she was somehow there.

"What do you mean?" I ask, puzzled.

"I haven't told you because I didn't want it to be real. I tried to ignore them, but lately they've been so overwhelming I can't block them out."

"Vale, what are you saying?" I ask, nerves creeping in.

"Inara, I have visions of other people's deaths. I'm forced to watch them die and then Abacus shows up. But this past month, Abacus has stayed in the same body and he seems unhinged. I thought they were just nightmares mixed with my visions or something, but I was watching when Cian saved you," Vale says, rocking back and forth in her seat.

"All of your paintings… they're the deaths you've seen?" I ask, finally piecing it all together.

"Yes."

"Oh my god, Vale. That's terrible. Maybe Cian will know a way to stop them," I say, remembering the journal he just got from his aunt—one full of secrets.

"Inara, there's more," she says sadly, reaching for both of my hands.

This has to be serious. All I can think about is calling Cian to tell him and trying to help Vale. I can't even imagine what this must be doing to her mentally.

"I have to show you something. I didn't want to believe it was real but take a look at what I painted this morning," Vale says, leading me to her latest canvas.

"Is that me?" I blurt out, shocked.

"Unfortunately, yes. I had hoped I was just talented. But I guess it's much more morbid than that."

"There's still more. Look at these. Abacus has been acting differently. I watched him take six beads from one person before they even answered," she says, showing me a dozen more paintings of Abacus collecting life beads in his hands.

I've never even considered that as a possibility. Vale has been watching Abacus collect souls for years right under my nose.

"Vale, I'm so sorry," I say and hug her tightly.

"Enough about me and my weird shit. Nothing we can do about it right now, and I need a new subject before I start crying. When's your next date?" she asks with a smirk, expertly dodging her own trauma—which I let her do, since I've been guilty of the same more times than I can count.

Our next date hasn't even crossed my mind. I've been so caught up in everything. But I suppose I need to start thinking about what's next. I shake my head at Vale in a way I know she understands. I'm not sure of anything right now. Between Cian awakening these feelings in me and finding out Vale is haunted by visions of death every day... I might break.

"Girls? Where are they?" Peggy calls out from the gallery floor.

We realize we've been back here way too long and quickly making our way out to the front. I try to refocus on the art, prep for the next showing... but then he texts me.

Cian: *I had an amazing night, sweetheart. I hope you weren't too late to work.*
Inara: *Me too. And thanks to you, I made it just in time. Thank you for the fancy lift.*
Cian: *You are very welcome, darling.*
Cian: *I want to see you again. Are you free tonight?*

I clutch my phone to my chest and smile so hard Vale picks up on it immediately, even from across the gallery helping a customer. I've never seen her wrap up a sale faster. Within minutes, she's walking over.

"Did he text you?"

I can't hide the excitement and happiness on my face. I really did enjoy our night, and I want to see him again too. I'm not imagining all that chemistry—he *has* to feel something too. The last jerk I dated waited a week to text me after our first date and even then, all he sent was, *'what's up,'* like that means anything. Cian just saw me a few hours ago and he's already texting.

"Yes, and he wants to see me tonight," I say with a smile so wide I couldn't hide it if you paid me.

"Not tonight. Make him wait for it," Vale says like she's the resident dating expert, and honestly, she kind of is.

Inara: *Tonight, I already have plans.*
Cian: *Dinner tomorrow at Aunt Clare's house?*
Cian: *I mean my house. I'm officially moving in today.*
Cian: *I want to cook dinner for you, to thank you for helping me finally get the nerve to come home. It means more than I can say.*

Before I even realize it, my fingers are already typing back. He has a way of doing that to me. A way of getting me to play right into his hands.

Inara: *Ok. I'll see you tomorrow night. And you're welcome. It was an amazing night.*

I can't believe I'm going to see him again tomorrow. Panic hits as I start thinking about the hundred outfits I have at home and how none of them feel right for a third date. He's already seen most of them over the past year anyway. I need something casual but flattering. Something that shows a little skin but not too much—it's all about balance. Gotta leave something to the imagination, but also remind him I'm a woman. The thought of Cian undressing me with his eyes sends warm tingles across my skin, and my face must be as red as my hair.

"Vale! Emergency. I need an outfit for tomorrow," I say, near desperate.

"You already texted him back? I can't leave you alone for a second. When's the second date?"

"Third date? Tomorrow night," I say, flashing her my phone.

Once Peggy heads out, we close the gallery a little early and head to the mall for an emergency shopping trip—mission:

perfect second/third date outfit. I'm excited… but also a little nervous. I'm nercited?

CHAPTER 10
CIAN: IMPATIENCE

I can't wait to see her tonight. I'm excited and a little nervous. I sit in the kitchen, staring at the clock on my new appliances while the delivery team finishes the install. I spent all day yesterday moving in, and most of today getting this place ready for our date. Bringing this house into the twenty-first century in less than two days was no small task. I even bought a few plants, because some movie I watched years ago said women feel more comfortable when a guy has plants in his home. I hope she likes it.

I glance at the clock again. Still an hour until she gets here; two if she's late like usual so I jump in the shower. The steam fogs the glass door, and the warm water melts away the stress clinging to me. I close my eyes and take a deep breath—then suddenly, that familiar chill creeps into my body.

The water turns cold as ice and stops midair. I see Abacus. Just as clearly as I did in the living room yesterday. He almost seems human, standing there watching me—like some stalker, not the one sent to reap my soul. But I don't remember dying. I don't feel different. Why is he here?

He looks the same as last time. I remember him as awkward and robotic, with fathomless eyes, but now his movements are fluid. His eyes are crystal blue. And the way he's just standing there, watching me... it's like he's the surprised one.

"Get a good look?" I ask him, just to make it clear I see him.

Then I act like he's not even there. I dry off with one of my new towels, step out, and get hit with an odd sense of déjà vu. I scan the bathroom. Nothing. Just my naked self in the mirror, alone. The house suddenly feels enormous. Maybe I imagined it. If Abacus was really here, he'd ask if I was ready and take a life. Maybe the water was just too hot. Either way, I better get dressed. Inara will be here soon.

After throwing on some clothes, I grab a beer and find Aunt Clare's journal to squeeze in a little research while I wait for her to arrive. I check the time, still forty-five minutes. My mind jumps back to the shower. I must be losing it. That bathroom moment felt real. It was like Abacus was right there, watching me. I settle into my new leather couch then startle and spill my beer because I see him again. He's standing across from me, still and silent.

Good thing I chose the coffee-colored couch, can't even tell it's wet. I look back up, but he's gone. My shield must be weakening. I need to check if Aunt Clare left any tips to strengthen it. I can't keep seeing him like this. I crack open the journal, and memories of Aunt Clare flood me...memories of being here with her, of how much I loved her. We spent more time together than I ever did with my parents. She always understood me.

I want to know everything she left behind. Especially these drawings. I'd bet anything this gem she colored is important. She took the time to color it so vividly. Each word I read brings a flicker of her back to life, only for it to fade just as fast. As I read another excerpt from her journal, I realize how young she was when she first encountered Abacus.

"Abacus, as I now call him, nearly got to me again tonight. I used to call him the executioner, but that name was too dark... too powerful and I'm done giving him that kind of hold over me. I still don't know what he wants, but I can't escape his reach no matter where I run or hide. He just appears, as if he was there all along, cloaked from sight until he chooses to confront me. I'll be alone the rest of my life if I don't figure this out. It feels like I'm running out of time."

I never knew she went through that. Where was my mom during all this? Clare had to figure out shielding on her own. She was incredible. I wish I could thank her for saving me more than once. I do like the name executioner, but Abacus sounds... less terrifying. Still. She must have seen something horrible to call him that.

She wrote her entire life down and it feels like I have a small piece of her that even death can't take from me. I can't stop reading. I turn the page and start something about a road trip when the doorbell rings.

"Inara!"

I lost track of time.

"Be right there!" I shout, rushing to the door.

The second I open it; my heart skips a beat. I'm caught off guard and instantly stunned. I don't know how, but she looks even more beautiful today.

Her lips are so enticing I can barely stop myself from kissing her right now. A cool breeze lifts the hem of her white sundress just enough to pull my eyes from her fiery red hair. The dress clings to her in all the right places, and the glimpse of cleavage is going to be dangerous tonight. My thoughts aren't pure—at all—I realize shaking my head to snap out of it.

"You are gorgeous. Please, come in, sweetheart," I say, stepping aside.

"Hi! Thanks, you clean up nice too," she replies, her voice soft and innocent.

As soon as she steps in, I pull her close and bring her lips to mine. Her arms wrap around my neck instantly, like she couldn't wait for this either.

"I missed you too," she whispers between kisses.

My heart races at the sound of her breathy voice. My hands explore her curves, and before I know it, I scoop her into one arm, slam the door shut, and press her against it. Her body slides down mine, her feet touch the floor, and I move in—palms flat on the door above her head, caging her in.

Her cheeks flush. She bites her lip. Her eyes lock onto mine and don't let go. She's nervous—and turned on. The mix is intoxicating. If I could freeze any moment, this would be it. She's so damn sexy. The way she plays the damsel when I know she's fierce underneath. She's the most beautiful woman I've ever seen.

My lips find her neck. I kiss, bite, just barely scraping teeth against skin. She moans and I lose all control. Her skin hums under my touch, her hips squirm in anticipation, as my hands roam over her curves. This dress leaves so much skin exposed and I want to strip it off and kiss every inch of it. I grab her hair gently, arching her back and pulling her body close so she can feel me.

"I need you," I whisper in her ear.

Her eyes go wide—she knows what I'm asking.

"Yes," she breathes, hips pushing into mine.

She kisses my neck, as her hands begin to roam beneath my shirt. She bites me, and I let out a growl I've never made before. My blood's on fire. I lift and her legs instinctively wrap around me. I carry her upstairs without breaking our kiss and gently lay her on the new bed.

"We can stop if you want. Just say the word and we'll go get dinner," I offer, holding my breath.

"Don't you dare stop. I need you, now," she whispers.

That's all I need. Shirt off. She pushes me back, stands, and turns so I can unzip her dress. I do, and it falls. She's in just lace...bra and panties. She unclasps her bra, and I'm the luckiest man alive. Suddenly she is pushing me toward the bed and I let her take control for a moment, then abruptly flip her, hover above, and begin to kiss my way up her body like I imagined doing downstairs.

Thighs, Navel. Breasts. Neck. Lips. I'm in heaven. I can't get enough of her. Every kiss leaves me wanting more. She runs her hands down my chest and lower. She wants me. I'm more than ready. When our bodies become one, it's like nothing else exists. This—this—feels right. Inara is my future.

...

Later, I'm holding her in my arms, feeling peace like I've never known. A warmth so strong fills me, I can barely believe what I'm thinking.

I love her... I'm in love with her. Being with her wakes me up. After a year of fighting each other, it feels amazing to be on the same side. I know this is fast, but I feel like I've known her forever. And life is short. I'd regret not being with her for every day we're given.

She's asleep, a satisfied smile on her lips. We never made it to dinner. She's going to be hungry. Honestly, I already am. Carefully, I slip my arm from beneath her head and replace it with a pillow. I pull the sheet up to cover her beautiful body, press a soft kiss to her forehead, and sneak downstairs, trying not to wake her.

I call the Mexican place down the street. Who can say no to a bean and cheese burrito or a cheese quesadilla? No one. And I already know she wants extra lettuce, tomato, and sour cream on hers. She's ordered the same thing a dozen times. I used to get annoyed at her complex orders, but now... it's kind of admirable. She knows exactly what she wants. And her way? It's usually delicious.

...

"Evening. Pick-up for Cian," I say to the hostess at the restaurant.

"Just a few more minutes and we'll have your order ready. Do you mind waiting over there, honey?" she says, pointing toward the crowded area near the kitchen.

"Of course," I reply, heading over.

She's probably barely out of high school. Still, hearing her call me "honey" makes me cringe, until she says it to the next customer, too. I hope Inara doesn't wake up while I'm gone. The thought of her waking to an empty bed, thinking I left her, floods me with anxiety. I need to get back to her. How long is this food going to take? They're usually so fast…

My thoughts distract me from the waiter rushing out with two large trays of food in his hands. He crashes into me at full speed. Suddenly, everything stops and I know what's happening even before I feel the cold chill crawl up my spine.

"Abacus," I say, spinning around and scanning the restaurant for the executioner.

I spot him, and I'm surprised to see he looks the same again—still some Irish guy with a hard jaw and jet-black hair. But something's different. Something has to have changed, because until recently, I don't recall Abacus ever reusing a body before.

"There you are," Abacus says, like he's been looking for me.

I don't comprehend how he can suddenly say anything other than his typical tagline. I'm stunned, frozen in this pocket of limbo with him and that can only mean one thing: he's here for one of my lives.

"I demand that you tell me everything you know about your abilities. You will help me regain what I lost. I don't have long, so start talking or you and the girl will die." His tone is commanding, threatening, and it catches me completely off guard.

"What? I literally don't know what's happening right now. Don't you have cosmic knowledge of all things or something like that? How could I possibly help you? I'm just an ordinary guy," I say, trying to recall anything from Aunt Clare's journal that might explain what's happening to me.

It's frustrating. All I want is to get back with this food before Inara wakes up. I'd give anything to be back in bed with her right now. I regret placing that order. I should've stayed.

"Tell me how you used my ring to save the girl, and maybe I won't kill you both," Abacus says, stepping closer.

Now I'm fucking pissed. First, he's here to take one of my lives, and now he's threatening to take them all, and worse, threatening the woman I love. A rage I haven't felt since the Marines flares to life. This is that waiter's fault. Images of Inara lying in my bed flash through my mind, and my blood boils at the thought of never seeing her again.

"I don't think you understand how this works, Abacus. You say, 'Are you ready?' and I say, 'No.' Then you disappear to wherever the fuck you go when you're not bothering me. Do your job. Goodbye and good riddance." I shout at the menacing reaper like I'm untouchable.

Probably not my best idea. Abacus seems unhinged. I feel his power press me down to one knee—some invisible force crushing my chest. He's actually visibly upset now. I don't know my next move, but telling death to screw off was clearly a mistake. Still, I'm in too deep to back out now.

My mind drifts back to that damn waiter... how he stole my moment of peace with Inara. I only have four lives left. This would knock me down to three. How can I have forever with her if I only have three?

What if this had been my last life? I'd be taken out by a clumsy waiter and never see Inara again. The thought enrages me further. Fire pumps through my veins, and I feel power hum at my fingertips. This is new—and I like it.

"Enough. You will tell me what I want, or I will take the girl's life after I kill you, which is going to happen no matter what you do now." Abacus raises his golden ring, reminding me who holds the power here.

"Tell me how I can become mortal again."

I feel it—the pull in my chest—like he's trying to force the truth out of me. But this time is different. He's not following the rules anymore... so why should I?

"Can't help you," I say flatly, keeping my answers short, protecting the journal and Aunt Clare's secrets.

He steps forward again, power radiating off him. A gust of wind swirls around us, even though we're inside. I'm out of time.

"This was the waiter's fault, not mine. It's his life you should take, not mine. Leave me alone!" I shout, exasperated, not realizing how powerful those words would be.

All at once, a strong force bursts from me and connects with the Abacus. My full attention locks on the ring in his hand. He's transfixed too—it starts to glow. A fiery red light, nearly blinding. Two rows of beads now rest on the abacus. One of the beads on the second row begins to glow crimson… then vanishes, leaving only a cloud of ash.

The second row now has eight beads left. I didn't even know that was possible. A million questions fly through my mind. Is this some trick? Is Abacus doing this to get what he wants? But I have no answers, only more confusion.

The top row still shows four lives left. Five spent. That first row has to be my lifeline, but if that's true… why didn't I lose a life just now?

"What is happening?" I ask aloud.

The waiter stumbles again but this time, he catches his balance and delivers the food without incident. Abacus is gone.

"Nice save!" someone shouts nearby.

As I look at the waiter, realization sinks in. The second lifeline—it gave a life for me. But it wasn't green like when I saved Inara, or when I helped Aunt Clare. It was red. A chill slides down my back, and a strange pulse surges through me. Pain stabs through my chest so sharp I think it's the end, but it vanishes as suddenly as it came. I stagger into the restroom, gripping the sink.

I turn the faucet and splash lukewarm water on my face. It smells like copper, but it helps settle me. I wipe my eyes and look at my reflection in the mir—

"My eyes! What the fuck?!"

Panic sets in. I feel lightheaded. These eyes in the mirror… they aren't mine. My warm brown eyes are gone, replaced by something unnatural. Cold. Blue. I forget the food. I bolt home. Maybe there's something in the journal—some answer. I creep into the house, careful not to wake Inara. No sign of her downstairs, so I assume she's still asleep.

I grab Aunt Clare's journal and flip back to the road trip, right where I left off. Sitting on the couch, I read like my life depends on it. And then an entry catches my eye.

"The abacus started to glow red, and a second row appeared in an instant. I didn't blink as I watched the wonder of the abacus. One had to be my row, which I knew had one bead remaining. But both of these lines are on their last life. I didn't know who the second belonged to—until it was too late.

I thought Abacus was doing it. But little did I know at the time... I had all the power. I later figured out it wasn't that easy. This power cost more than I was willing to pay."

She saw the same thing I did. She used someone else's life. If she hadn't... I might never have met her. But she killed someone.

"Oh fuck. What have I done?" I whisper.

The price is steep for using someone else's life, even by accident. I don't want this. I didn't mean to take his life. Maybe if I find Abacus... maybe I can give it back? Maybe that would work? But my mind keeps circling back to those blue eyes. His eyes. I stole his life. I'm such an idiot. Why did I say it should have been the waiter?

Apparently, death works in absolutes. I took an innocent life. And now, I'm forever marked for it. My eyes are just the beginning. Aunt Clare wrote that her eyes were forever changed, too. She warned me...use another's life, and your soul will carry the stain.

"I'm so sorry," I whisper.

The weight of my actions settles over me like wet concrete. I took a life. In war, I took lives too but that was different. That was in defense. This? This was a curse. Aunt Clare would be so disappointed in me but I know she'd still hug me. She'd still help me fix it. She was always calm and kind when things went wrong. I wish she were here. My stomach knots. All I want is to crawl back into bed and pretend this didn't happen.

"Inara." I nearly forgot—she's still here.

I can't let her see me like this. I grab my sunglasses and slide them on, hiding the monster behind the lenses, and slip into the downstairs bathroom. I won't let her see what I've become.

CHAPTER 11
CIAN: UNDER PRESSURE

"Cian, where are you?" Inara's voice calls out, searching for me.

Aunt Clare's journal talks about the darkness that comes with taking a life—how it consumes you no matter your intentions. I can't picture her being overtaken by that. She was always so kind, so calm. She never let on that she was carrying trauma like this. She must have found a way to fight it... to hold onto herself. I need to keep reading. I need to find the cure before I can face Inara. But doubt and guilt flood in, drowning any sense of reason.

I stay in the bathroom frantically scanning the pages for anything that could fix this. I should tell her what happened. Inara would probably want to help. She'd want to solve this together. But what if I hurt her? I can't risk it. The darkness I unleashed might claim her next. She'd see it the moment she looked at my face.

"This is it. The end is near, and I can feel the walls closing in. I've tried to find a cure. I've tried to stop using my abilities to cheat death. But every time Abacus came, I did it again. I sacrificed someone else for more time. I drove this stolen car into the middle of nowhere, and when it finally died, I hiked deep into the woods. I think I'm ready."

She thought she was going to die. But the date on the page is from over twenty years before I was even born. What happened to her after that? The next pages are torn out. She must've used her power again to survive. If she couldn't resist it after all that time..., what chance do I have?

I'm no hero. A hero wouldn't have taken that waiter's life. That was selfish. Reckless. Inara deserves better, so much better. I can't bear the thought of her looking at me and seeing what I've become.

"Cian, this is not funny! Where are you?" Inara's voice cuts through the silence again. She's opening doors now. I can hear the worry creeping in.

Maybe I could just text her that I had to step out—

"Ring! Ring! Ring!"

My phone betrays me. Damn traitor. I sigh, shove the journal on the counter, and open the door. No more hiding. Time to face the music. As I move toward her voice, I glance at the mirror by the entry and double-check that my sunglasses are still in place.

"Cian, I was starting to worry." She gives a nervous laugh.

"If this was some kind of hide-and-seek thing, you forgot to tell me first."

Her smile almost breaks me. It's so sweet it makes me want to rip these glasses off and pull her into my arms.

"Sorry," I lie, too easily.

"I thought I remembered something Aunt Clare kept in the hall closet. Guess I was wrong."

The words roll off my tongue like I've been lying my whole life. Maybe I have. I avoid her eyes, feeling myself pull away, retreating into the guilt and anger. Even now, I can see the abacus glowing red, reminding me of what I did. Of what I am.

"Are you okay? You seem... different." She's watching me too closely, like she can see right through the lenses.

"Inara, you need to leave." My voice is low and sharp.

"I'm sorry. I can't do this."

I usher her toward the door, practically tossing her purse at her. I close the door behind her without another word. What the hell am I doing? A voice inside screams at me to stop. But I know I'm doing the right thing. If she stays, I'll drag her into this darkness with me. I'm a dead man walking. I can't take her down with me.

"Cian, wait! Can we talk about this?" she pleads, trying to push back inside.

But I overpower her easily. I toss her the last of her things, slam it shut and lock it. No goodbye. No explanation. Just locked her out so she wouldn't learn the truth. The look on her face—pain, confusion, betrayal—it guts me. She's going to hate me. But at least she'll live. At least she'll have the chance to find someone who won't ruin her, who won't use her to stay alive. I lean my back against the door and slide down to the floor, breath shallow, heart hollow. She deserved better. I was a fool to ever think I could be that man.

"You know what, Cian? Fuck you!" she yells through the door.

"I guess you're just another asshole crayon-eater after all! Lose my number. Don't show your face at group again. I can't believe you just wanted to sleep with me. You're a pig!"

The words hit harder than a punch. I sit in silence, the cool floor grounding me while my world crumbles. We had something real. And I destroyed it. I need to stay away from all of them now. They've been my family this past year but they'd never forgive me for what I've become. Vale would probably stab me herself when she finds out.

Keep them safe. That phrase keeps repeating in my head. Don't lose your nerve now, Marine. I want to run after Inara. I want to tell her the truth. But instead, I force myself to stand, not for her, but for the journal. Maybe there's still something in there, something that can fix this.

"Cian, please don't judge me too harshly. I deserve it, but I hope you'll understand one day. This journal helped me cope

with all the death, the grief, and this curse we possess. If you ever feel lost, know that there's still hope as long as you have one life left and you have love in your heart. Loving you was the cure for me. You were the best part of my life. Don't blame yourself for telling your parents. This could only end one way, my sweet boy. I want to tell you what to do next but the truth is that you must find your own path and find a way to master your power so it does not consume you."

I read her words over and over. She went through so much. She left this behind for me to do better. How is love the cure? Who would love me now? I'll just disappear. Live out what time I have left in peace and solitude like she tried. I am not going to put anyone else at risk.

"While love is the cure; the only way to fully protect others from your ability is to keep your distance. If you stay, the temptation will always exist. You'll use your power without even thinking to save yourself. You'll kill others to save them. If you don't control your abilities then you will have to answer to Fate.

Your Uncle Jay was a good man. He gave everything for us. When your father died, I was lost in grief and was hopeless. Jay's love kept me afloat... and gave me the strength to bring you into the world. The more you use the gift, the harder it becomes to resist. Eventually, it becomes instinct. Still, I want you to find love and to live as close to a normal life as you can. It won't be easy but nothing in life worth doing is."

I blink, stunned, as the next part hits me like a freight train.

"Jay gave his life so that you could be born. You were saved by a mortal man with no power—just his courage and his love for me. You must do better than I did. Guard the secrets I left behind and don't let anyone find the Gem of Life. It's too dangerous. It will lead to Fate stepping in and destroying who ever holds it or worse. And Cian, please forgive your mother. I passed this curse on to you and doubt I'll live to see you graduate. I love you. I wanted to keep you, but I was out of time. Jay convinced me to stop using my power so that you might live safely. You saved me, my son. I wanted you to have a real home. One I never did. Please forgive me for not telling you sooner. Your father and you were the best part of my life. Guard your heart well. And remember... if you're ever out of time, go to the basement. Everything you need can be found. You are stronger than you realize and if anyone from an organization called the Order shows up, run! They only show themselves if there is a threat to the balance and will kill everyone in a mile radius to safeguard their secrets and what they think is the proper balance of life and death."

The journal slips from my hands, landing with a soft thud. I sit there, stunned, barely breathing. She was my mother. All this time, she lied. Aunt Clare... was my mom. The weight I've carried for years—this guilt about loving her more than my parents—shifts. And now it all makes sense. But with that truth comes something new. A whole lot more sorrow. She knew she was on borrowed time and was going to die, so she gave me away, thinking it would spare me. But now I know the pain of losing a mom twice and never even knowing my dad.

"Aun—Clare."

The pain of her death hits me all at once, deep and raw. Clare was my mom—that's why I have the same curse. Memories of our life together keep flooding in, and that emptiness I've always carried around starts to feel... full somehow. I head to the kitchen and grab a beer. As I reach for it, I catch my reflection in the glass. My eyes—her eyes—just like I used to wish for as a kid.

"I get it now. How awful it must've been to hear me wish for something so twisted and tragic."

I say it to a mother who now only exists in memories and scribbled words on a page. The first beer takes the edge off. The second one gives me the nerve to pick the journal back up.

"The basement?" I say out loud.

I always wondered what she kept down there. She kept it locked; saying she stored the monsters she caught over the years down there. I figured it was just boring adult stuff—Christmas decorations or old clothes. But now, I have to get in there. Where'd she leave the keys? I rush out to the shed and grab the first tool I can find—a rusty crowbar. I bolt back inside and head for the basement door. Deep breath. I wedge the crowbar into the frame and push. With a groan and a crack, the lock gives way. The door creaks open. I step inside.

Why didn't I come home sooner? That thought lands like a gut punch. I picture Inara and imagine her telling Vale what a jerk I've been. Then the two of them taking shots and cursing my name while planning my public shaming. The stairs moan under my weight as I descend, each one louder than the last. Somehow, by some miracle, the light still works.

Then—

"Shit!"

The bulb explodes. I slip down the last three stairs and land hard on my ass. Grumbling, I haul myself up, using a dusty filing cabinet. My hand lands on what I think is a lamp. When it flickers on, light spills into the room and I swear I can see her for a second. Clare. Sitting at the desk like she's treasure hunting.

There's a massive map pinned to the wall with pages, photos, and strings of green and red connecting them like some conspiracy web. She lived two lives… and this one? I knew nothing about it. I step toward a group of trunks that look like they came from Atlantis with gold accents. It's easily the oldest things I have ever seen. Carefully, I open the first one. The lid groans.

"Wow… I really didn't know you at all," I whisper to the ghost of my mother.

Weapons. Enough to start a war. I open trunk after trunk—assault rifles, handguns, knives. And then…

"A freaking sword!" The Marine in me immediately connects with it.

Swords have always been my favorite. But why would Clare need a sword with all these guns? Especially one this beautiful—custom, possibly ceremonial, very expensive. This thing belongs in a museum. I lift it up into the light. The craftsmanship is unreal. It feels alive. That icy chill runs up my spine. I glance around, expecting Abacus. Nothing. The hilt has a blue gem embedded in it. It looks just like a bead from the golden abacus if I didn't know better. I stare in awe as the gem begins to glow, blue light pulsing and surrounds the blade. I reach out and—stupidly—touch it.

It slices my finger like it's nothing. It's been years since I've held a sword. Mostly drills and ceremonies in the Corps. But this? This feels more natural in my hands than any rifle ever did. I swing it around, effortless. It hums as it cuts through the air. I feel powerful. Invincible. I forget why I came down here.

I don't want to let go of this thing. I need to keep it. Why would Clare have this? Why does it feel like it was made for me? I feel like that guy from the old Marine Corps commercial, pulling the sword from the stone, slaying dragons, fire all around him. That commercial might be the reason I chose the Marines in the first place. Not that I'd admit it to anyone.

"Why did I come down here?"

The echo of my voice bounces off the basement walls, snapping me out of the trance. I sheath the sword and set it down on the desk. The second I let go, the sorrow crashes back in…everything I'm holding inside. The weight of hurting Inara. The guilt from stealing a life. And the truth that Clare was actually my mother.

I wonder about my father. Did he have abilities too? What happened to him? I search the filing cabinets. Most are filled with cryptic documents that have no labels, no order I can recognize, no page numbers. Thousands of documents. I slump into a wooden chair. Dust explodes upward and attacks my nose. I sneeze so hard it echoes.

"What am I supposed to do now?" I ask the room, defeated.

I rock back in the chair and hear a loud crack before I hit the cold concrete. Perfect. I broke the damn chair. I can hear Clare scolding me already.

"What's that?"

From this angle, I spot a box tucked under the desk. It's dirty, ancient-looking. A note is taped discreetly to the side. I carefully pull it out and unfold the faded paper. She left me another message.

"Cian. Son, I know you must be upset, and I wish I could be there to take this journey with you. But alas, my time has run out. If you're reading this, then please let me go and move forward, even if that means forgetting me. If you are happy and still avoiding the chaos that plagues our bloodline leave now and never come back. I mean it, stop reading and run. The knowledge contained in this letter is heavily guarded and comes with a great responsibility.

I never thought you'd inherit the curse; it usually skips generations. I planned for you to have a long, ordinary life free of this burden, but if you are still reading this then my son it is already too late for normal.

In this box, you'll find the locations of the most powerful items in the world, they are scattered amongst my safe houses to prevent anyone person from obtaining them all. Some are already stored safely here; I am certain you will find the sword. It has a certain call to it and will keep you safe. If any of these items fall into the wrong hands, it will bring about the end of days. Not just for our realm, but potentially all of them. Protect these treasures and secrets Cian. Burn it if you must.

These items and secrets have been passed down for generations. From the first of us to my great grandfather, to me, and now to you. Our bloodline traces back to the first mortal ever to be gifted this power. Be the man you're destined to be. You have more power than any of us, I saw it that night when you saved me. A storm is coming. You can save the world or be the end of all life. Choose well and know I love you which ever path you walk. You gave me hope when I was lost and woke something in me that I thought was gone forever.

The most dangerous of all these treasures is the green gem of life. It has the power to give life to those who have lost it but always at a cost. Fate will surely stop anyone who uses it, but please make sure to keep that one locked away. It's a life bead that was removed from the first death's abacus. Each death has had their own unique abacus which becomes an extension of themselves and manifests from their power. I know this is too much to put on you in a letter but it is important you know. The Order only shows themselves if they see you as an ally or a threat to the natural order and balance to the universe. Don't trust them and never let them know of your full abilities. You were always mine and always will be. Stay safe. Protect our secrets. And trust those who you love. I have found love is stronger than my fear and if I had trusted it sooner who knows the path I would have taken. There are others like us—you must avoid them even though they are related by blood they will not recognize you as their family and eliminate you as a threat. My great grandfather left our ancestors behind when he was a small boy and had to hide most of his life because of it. Everything you need to know is in these files and my journal. The key to the filing system is in the desk drawer. I love you and remember if you need help look to the map."

I stare at the letter in disbelief. This is too much. My head starts to ache and the room spins. A thousand questions flow through my mind. There are others like me? I slowly open the box, half expecting it to explode. Inside: a map, a compass, another small journal, a dozen precise gems, some sketches of the green abacus bead and a very old candy bar. Definitely expired. Also… a watch. It's sleek, silver, and masculine. Doesn't look like it ever belonged to Clare. My father's, maybe?

The watch is still running. After all these years, how? The time's accurate. There's a crystal in place of the twelve, and when I strap it on, I swear it glows blue for a second. Weird. I examine the drawings next. These aren't Clare's...they're old, sealed in plastic. A name at the bottom: Jameson Case. Who is that? And what does he have to do with all this?

I lean against the wall, mind still spinning. Resurrection is real. The green gem is a life bead, from death itself. How did Clare get all of this? She tried to give me a normal life. But I messed that up. Still, she asked me to safeguard these secrets and treasures. Should I just burn it? What if there is a cure to cancer in here or something?

I read the letter again and open the desk drawer to figure out her filing system. I pull out a master key that should help me figure all of this out, that is once I figure out how to read it. My eyes start to droop. I keep reading the same sentence over and over, fighting sleep. But the weight of it all is too much.

I just need to rest... then maybe I can figure out what comes next....

CHAPTER 12
INARA: SCORNED

My mind is spiraling, and all I see is red.

"That bastard!"

I can't believe I fell for all of his lies. I thought he was genuine, that he actually cared about me. I feel so stupid. How did I not see this coming? He was charming and kind, never pressured me. And now, just like that, he pulls away. If I see him again, I swear I'll give him a piece of my mind.

My blood pressure's climbing…I can tell because my face is tingling, and I can't feel my nose. I need backup. I text Vale to meet me for a drink. My thoughts circle back to Cian and his stupid, handsome face. The nerve of that jerk, kicking me out like that—after the most amazing night of my life. I shouldn't even be thinking about it, but God, it was spectacular.

My knees go weak just remembering that toe-curling action. His touch was so tender, but I could feel his raw strength when he held me. He treated every part of me like I was the most important thing in the world.

Ugh. Obviously not. I'm so mad I could scream.

"Shit. I forgot to hit send."

Inara: *Urgent! Meet for drinks at The Pint. I need you.*
Vale: *On my way now.*
Vale: *Do we need a shovel or champagne?*
Inara: *Whiskey + a shovel.*
Vale: *Oh, shit! 15 out.*

I knew she'd come. Vale always shows up for me. How could Cian do this after everything we shared this past week? I thought I was finally seeing the real him. But no gentleman would act the way he just did. And yet, he did give up a life for me. He opened up about his past. None of it adds up. He couldn't have faked all of that, right? I'm usually great at reading people. I thought he genuinely cared. Was he really that desperate to sleep with me—enough to sacrifice a life?

God. That's... kind of hot. A man willing to die just to be with you? I mean, if I'm gonna be bought, a life feels like a better price than most. I can't stop thinking about his smug face when he kicked me out, wearing sunglasses inside, like a creep. Who even does that? He couldn't even look me in the eye. Total coward. I replay the moment at least a hundred times while I wait at The Pint, our favorite local bar. I'm on my third drink by the time Vale walks in and immediately wraps her arms around me.

"I will cut him. I'm assuming this is because Cian did something stupid," Vale says, spot on, of course.

"Maybe. For now, can we just drink?" I reply, trying to dodge the conversation.

"Excuse me! Can a girl get a drink over here?" She calls to the bartender, who's finishing up with another customer.

I sigh, dropping my head onto the cool bar for a second. I second guess each and every life choice I made that put me here.

"I saw Cian again tonight. And… we couldn't keep our hands off each other. From the moment he opened the door—Vale, it was incredible. Like, earth-shattering, this can't be real, stardust-falling kind of passion."

"That's amazing! I knew you two were perfect for each other." Vale claps her hands with joy until the reality sinks in.

"Wait… I'm not hearing a downside yet. What happened?"

"Then he flipped. Just—switched off. Tossed me out like I was trash. After everything we shared, after how connected I thought we were. He made me feel used. Betrayed." Tears sting my eyes before I can stop them.

"I'll kill him! Bartender! Two shots, whiskey!" Vale slams her hand down.

She turns to me, softer now.

"What do you need?" she asks, hugging me tight.

I shake my head, wiping away the tears. I know she's friends with him too. Probably thought he walked on water until five minutes ago, but she's ready to go to war for me anyway. That image makes me laugh...Vale storming his place, full-on vengeance mode, slamming her small but mighty fists of fury into him like a professional.

"Something isn't sitting right with me," I say as she pays for the shots and orders two more.

"Nothing about this is right. That asshole isn't getting away with this. I'm so sorry I ever thought he was anything but a dirtbag," Vale huffs, wrapping her arm around my shoulders.

"No, I mean... the way he acted. When I found him—he was hiding from me and wearing sunglasses. Indoors. At night. It was like I woke up to someone else in his body. Even last year, when we fought constantly, he never treated me this cold. He was never cruel. Vale, I think something's wrong with him. Is it dumb if I go back to check on him? I know I should be pissed, but I can't shake this feeling."

Her expression shifts, brows furrowing. Concern creeps in. Yeah. Sunglasses in a dark house, hiding like a kid playing hide-and-seek? Rushing me out like that? Something's off.

"Maybe something happened when I was asleep or maybe he's overwhelmed. He did just find that journal his aunt left him, and he's moved into her house."

"Abacus," I whisper.

"Maybe he showed up and scared Cian. Or maybe Cian found something in the journal that worried him. Or… I don't know, maybe this thing between us just moved too fast and he panicked."

I look at Vale, hoping she'll validate even one of those theories.

"Inara, I love you. So, I'm saying this with care," she begins, giving me a stern look.

"He needs a doctor, because he must be seriously damaged if he let you go. Let alone kicked you out. But yeah… it's weird. Something could have happened, or he may have just liked the chase."

I smile through the chaos in my head. That's the thing about Vale. She always supports me, even when I'm being irrational, and protects me, sometimes from myself. Every time.

"Okay, yes, Cian's a bit of a hot mess. I'll give you that. But maybe his feelings scared him. Maybe he's trying to protect me, like an idiot, by pushing me away. Maybe he's hurt. Or maybe Abacus really did show up. There are a dozen explanations that make more sense than him just being over me. I mean, look at this." I gesture dramatically at my body, confidence boosted by the third shot of whiskey.

Vale just laughs and raises her glass. "To dumb, beautiful men with hero complexes and poor communication skills."

"To annoying men, whiskey, and bad decisions," I reply, clinking her glass.

I reposition on the barstool and swipe my hair out of my eyes so I can fully see Vale's perfect smile.

"Another round, bartender and make it a double!" I shout.

I'm not prepared for shots four and five, but the conversation suddenly shifts back to me and Cian sleeping together. Vale leans in, hungry for every detail. Images of Cian flood my mind, and just like that, I'm flushed and squirming in my seat. I press my knees together, tightly.

"His body was all muscle, and he was exactly as commanding as I imagined… and hoped. His confidence was so hot, but also calming. I felt safe. I melted when he asked if I wanted to be his good girl," I blurt, practically telling the whole bar.

"I knew he had it in him," Vale grins, sliding another shot toward me.

I can't even remember the last time a memory made me squeeze my thighs together like that but damn, it was the best I've ever had.

"It was… amazing," I admit, softer this time.

Just as quickly as the heat builds from the memory, a cold chill slips in. A knot forms where the warmth had been. What if he really did just use me and toss me aside?

"There's just an intensity with him that I've never felt before," I say, trying to untangle my thoughts.

"He makes me feel better than I ever have. I thought I made him feel the same way. I was so happy, but now I wonder if I'm just romanticizing everything. What if it really was just sex for him? What if I didn't mean anything at all?" My words spill out fast as I start to spiral again.

"No good ever comes from falling down a rabbit hole like that," Vale says calmly, wrapping me in a much-needed hug.

"Maybe he just got spooked by his feelings and tried to push you away. Cian might flirt, sure, but I've never seen him use women. Not like that. Not without being upfront about it."

She orders two waters so we can slow down and sober up a bit. The scent of her coconut body spray makes me ache for the beach. I can almost taste the piña colada on my lips, feel the waves crashing into me, the salty air, seagulls calling overhead. My happy place: white sand, crystal blue water, and a good book in my lap.

"I need to get out of here. Maybe... Key West for the weekend. You in?" I ask, already planning the trip in my head.

But before she can answer, the bar plunges into darkness. Someone cries out behind us, startled.

"Sorry, folks, power's out, which means we're closing up early tonight," the bartender shouts.

As people start filing out, a man bursts through the front door, nearly knocking a couple over.

"Come check this shit out!" He yells.

"Holy cow!" Someone gasps from outside.

Vale and I look at each other, then push through the crowd. What we see stops us cold. The entire city is blanketed in darkness for as far as we can see. Not even emergency lights are on. The only illumination comes from lightning streaking violently across the sky—way too close for comfort—and it is tinted purple, which somehow makes it even more unsettling.

"I've never seen a storm this bad. If everything is out, it had to have hit a transformer or maybe even the power station," Vale says, gripping my hand so we don't get separated in the moving crowd.

"So... you see it too? I thought maybe I was just drunk for a sec," I say, trying to get a better view as the lightning cracks again.

Then, screeching tires. A crash. We both jerk our heads toward the sound and see two cars smashed together in the intersection.

"Boom!" Another bolt hits a block away, lighting a building on fire.

"We should get home before things get worse," I say, heart pounding.

"No streetlights mean more accidents are coming. This lightning is way too close. Thank you for being here, Vale." I pull her into a quick hug and start sending her toward her place.

"Of course. You know I'm always here for you. Want to come to my place for the night? Ride out whatever this is together?" She offers, forgetting for a second that I've got my fur baby waiting at home.

"I would but Spencer's all alone, and he hates thunderstorms. I'll call you when I get home, if the power is still on." I say, glancing at my dead phone, weird.

"Be safe. Love you. Send a smoke signal if you need me," she says, making her way through the crowd.

Her place is just a few blocks up.

...

It takes an hour, but I finally make it home in one piece. I glance up, power's still on here. Thank God. As I open the door, Spencer nearly tackles me, tail wagging and full of chaotic energy. He demands to go out, immediately.

"Hey, my chocolate baby. Let's get you outside to potty and then it's dinner time," I chuckle, clipping on his leash.

He jumps and licks with the kind of enthusiasm only a dog can have. Honestly, if Cian greeted me like this next time, I wouldn't complain. What the hell am I thinking? Cian literally pushed me away.

"Spencer! No more men. Just you and me, buddy," I say as we head outside.

We walk the block, and the sirens are getting louder in the distance. The storm's still dancing overhead with lightning flashing, but still no rain. My mind drifts back to Cian. Is he safe right now?

Suddenly, Spencer yanks hard, nearly pulling my arm from the socket, dragging me toward an alley I have zero interest in investigating.

"Spencer, stop it. Come on buddy, let's go home and get your food," I say, trying to reel him in.

He skids to a halt at the edge of the alley, fur bristling, a deep, guttural growl rumbling from his chest. It rattles in my ears and chills my spine. I've never seen him act like this.

My brain flashes with all the things that could be lurking in that alley and none of them end well. Spencer's not a big dog, but he's fearless. Still, I scoop him up and head straight home before we find out what had him so freaked. My heart pounds as I slam the door shut and double-check the lock.

"What was that?" I ask Spencer, knowing full well he can't answer me.

I feed him, then sink into the fluffy couch and turn on the TV, hoping the news can explain any of this. Breaking news flashes across the screen, interrupting everything. I flip the channel—then another—and another. Every single one is reporting the same emergency broadcast:

"Ladies and gentlemen, we regret to inform you that, for your own safety, you should remain indoors. The power grid across the city is failing, and we're experiencing rolling blackouts. At this time, the cause is still unknown. If you're hearing this broadcast, we urge you to find a safe place and stay there. The storm is intensifying, and cities across the country are reporting similar conditions: a widespread lightning event unlike anything we've seen, accompanied by blackouts.

Now... I don't want to cause panic, but I feel it's my duty to report what we're hearing. There have been disturbing accounts of **sudden, unexplained deaths** *happening all over the world. In some cases, entire buildings have been found with no survivors. The CDC is actively quarantining affected areas as they're discovered, but I cannot stress this enough, stay inside. Stay alert. I've been advised not to say this, but the truth is, no one knows what's going on."*

My hands shake as the weight of it settles in. This isn't just happening here. It's everywhere. The whole world. And that anchorman sounded rattled. Then I remember something Cian told me once, about his time in the Marines. That sometimes, before moving into hostile territory, they'd cut the power. A blackout before the storm. Is that what this is? Are we under attack?

I can picture him now, probably calm as ever, sitting in his big empty house, eating candy and loading his guns, like it's just another Tuesday. What a handsome jerk. Still, I have to text him. I can't think of anyone better than him in a situation like this.

Inara: *Have you seen the news?*
Inara: *Can we talk?*
Inara: *Cian, I'm scared. Please respond.*
Inara: *I don't know what happened between us, but at least let me know you're alive. Even if you're an asshole, that doesn't mean I have to be.*
Inara: *I guess I really was just a conquest to you. Fine. I'll stop texting. I still hope you're safe, even though you hurt me... Dick!*

...

His silence says more than words ever could. Still, I can't stop thinking about him. Can't stop worrying that maybe, just maybe, he's in danger. Maybe by morning, this heartbreak will sting a little less. Maybe the world won't be falling apart anymore. I scoop up my pup and crawl into bed, burying myself under the covers, clinging to the small warmth he brings. Tomorrow has to be better. It just has to be.

CHAPTER 13
CIAN: THE STORM

The loud crash of thunder jolts me awake. I blink into darkness and realize I've fallen asleep in the cold basement. I reach for my phone, screen lighting up just enough to reveal the time and a flood of missed texts from Inara, plus a few from Vale, Charlie, and John.

"Shit." It's already 7:00 AM. She sent those messages last night. God, I hope she's okay.

I was already an asshole, and then I left her terrified and alone during all this chaos. It must have been bad if everyone was trying to reach me. She probably hates me now. Rubbing my palms over my face, I try to shake off the sleep. I need coffee before I can respond to any of them. As I climb the stairs toward my fuel of choice, my thoughts stay locked on Inara. I can't believe she even tried to talk to me after the way I threw her out.

She shouldn't be around me now. I'm too dangerous. If I respond, I'll just end up hurting her again. I have to stay strong. I have to resist the urge to get her back. My mind drifts back to the armory Clare stockpiled down here. Guns, boxes of ammo, bulletproof vests… and that sword. Why did she have all this? What was she really involved in?

I know I'm not supposed to tell anyone about this, but part of me wants to, especially Inara. About the gem. About how it can resurrect someone... or destroy everything. I glance outside. No sun. Just lightning. Endless, pulsing lightning across a black sky. Is this still just a storm? Did we lose power everywhere? I open the front door. The world is still wrapped in darkness, split only by streaks of lightning tearing across the sky like it's being ripped in half.

I remember the small generator downstairs and decide to try it. Proud of myself for getting it running... after only an hour, no less. Now I've got power. And somehow, thanks to Clare (or some divine miracle), the internet's still working. Seriously, Clare... how?

I push past the disbelief and flip on the news. It's worse than Inara said. Total chaos. Rolling blackouts. Riots. Looting. Fear in every reporter's voice. Bodies showing up everywhere—no signs of what killed them. Only Abacus could be behind this much death. Is this my fault? Did I unbalance something when I took that life? The journal said balance is key. If we use our powers to cheat Fate... the consequences are unpredictable. I need to see Inara. He threatened her if I didn't help him. If Abacus is causing all this, she's in danger. The whole group is.

Cian: *Inara, I'm so sorry I didn't respond last night. Please tell me you're okay.*

Cian: *I know you have no reason to trust me, but I care about you. And I think Abacus is behind all this. He might be coming for you and the others to hurt me.*

Inara: *I hate you. But... I'm also really scared, and I'm glad you're not dead. You owe me an explanation and it better be a good one. Why does Abacus want to hurt you?*

Cian: *I owe you a thousand apologies. But right now, we need to get you somewhere safe. Can you make it to my house? I've got a literal war bunker in the basement. We should bring Vale, John, and Charlie too.*

Inara: *I'm on my way. I'll bring Spencer. I haven't been able to reach anyone else since last night. Most people don't have power, and cell towers keep going down all over.*

Cian: *Okay. I'll keep trying to reach them. Be careful, sweetheart.*

Cian: *Hey gang! If you get this, come to my house ASAP. It's safe. Watch your back. I think Abacus is behind all of this and he may be targeting us.*

...

I don't know what I'm doing. She should be running in the opposite direction, not coming here. But I can't fight this need to see her. To make sure she's safe. Logically, it makes sense to gather the group here. I've got supplies, weapons… Clare's research. There's even a cabinet labeled "Out of Time." Fitting. Her note said everything I need is down here and I think I can read this master key now.

Clare documented everything about our power and so much more. There are things in here that seem supernatural. Clare lived far beyond a normal lifespan. While I wait for Inara, I dive into her notes, hoping to find answers—hoping I'll learn how to tell the woman I love that I'm a ticking time bomb. I think I caused this, all of it. When I accidentally took that waiter's life, I must have thrown the universe off balance.

How do I explain that to her? The thought of facing Inara is more terrifying than this global apocalypse. I'd rather face the end of the world than see the disappointment in her eyes when I tell her what I've done.

Inara: *Just a few minutes out.*

Cian: *Doors unlocked. Come on in.*

I hear her gently knock and then open the door and let herself in, her sweet voice calling out for me.

"Cian, are you here?"

"Inara!" I answer, already on the stairs.

"I'm in the basement—coming up."

When I see her, I swear she looks even more beautiful than the last time. I reach for her free hand. She pulls away.

Still mad. Of course. I deserve it. Spencer must agree based on the glare he is giving me right now.

"I'm sorry," I say.

"I know that's not enough, and it doesn't fix anything, but I panicked. I did something stupid. Inara… you're the most important person in the world to me. I regret lying to you. I regret pushing you away. I—"

She interrupts me with a kiss, pulling me down to her level, lips crashing into mine… urgent, fierce. I guess that means I'm forgiven. I pushed her away, and now I'm pulling her back in. I'm selfish. I know this is going to end badly for her. But maybe I can keep her safe. Clare said love is the only hope and I have fallen for this gorgeous woman. She said I'm stronger than she ever was. I promise, Inara—I'll keep you safe. No matter the cost.

"Don't think you're off the hook." She scans my face, then locks eyes with me.

I stand frozen, searching for the right words, but my brain's coming up empty.

"I'm sorry. I promise, no more lies. You are—"

"Your eyes!" She interrupts; her voice laced with shock.

"What happened to them?"

Shit. This isn't how I wanted to tell her.

"I know… I look like a monster. It happened yesterday when I went out to get us food while you slept. I don't even fully understand it myself, but I'll try to explain, for you." I take her hand and lead her into the kitchen.

"Want something to drink? Eat?" I offer, stalling for time.

"No. But I would love some answers," she snaps, all fire and bite like only she can.

I take a breath. "While I was waiting, a waiter tripped and ran into me. Then Abacus appeared but he was different. He talked. He threatened me and anyone I care about if I didn't help him. I got angry. I should've lost a life right then, but instead, I... I took one. Somehow, I used my ability without meaning to and stole the waiter's life."

I brace for her reaction—expecting anger, disgust, fear. She surprises me.

"Abacus? What do you mean you took his life? You spoke to him? Why are your eyes blue?"

"All good questions," I nod.

"And I'll answer them. But first, the truth—about me, my family, and the basement."

I spill everything. The family legacy. The hidden armory. The journal. My powers. Clare's secrets.

"I didn't mean to do it," I say, voice lower now.

"I want to fix it and give the life back, if I can. That's why my eyes look like this. I didn't want you to see what I've become. Clare warned me that to protect the one I love… I had to stay away."

I turn away, unable to look at her. She's quiet. Too quiet. I can feel her gaze drilling into the back of my skull. I've lost her. I deserve to.

"Cian, did you just say you love me?" Her voice cuts through the silence with a soft smirk.

I freeze. "I, uh… I did. Yes."

"I love you, sweetheart. So much." I say again with certainty.

She lets out a sharp breath.

"What the hell, you jerk. Why didn't you trust me sooner?" Her tone softens.

"I was pissed, yeah. I thought you were just using me. It hurt that you lied, that you didn't trust me enough to talk to me. But… I get it. Our lives aren't exactly normal. And you're going through more than most."

She steps closer and places a hand on my shoulder. "I think I love you too, by the way."

Suddenly, we're both laughing and I'm flooded with relief, nerves, adoration. I pull her into my arms. I steal a kiss, slow and deep, trying to pour everything I feel into it. I was a fool to push her away.

"I'm scared of what I'm becoming," I admit.

"What if I steal your life? I couldn't live with that."

"Stop it." Her tone turns firm.

"You're not a monster. You're fifty percent an asshole, sure, but not a monster. Would a monster feel this guilty?" She grabs my jaw and makes me look into her eyes.

"Cian. Look at me."

I want so badly to believe her. But the storm outside reminds me we don't have the luxury of time right now. Spencer barks, breaking the spell, she has me under. With tail wagging I let him out into the yard to run.

"There's more," I say.

"Clare... she was my mom. She arranged the adoption and kept the truth from me. I found another note in the basement. Also, when I said it was a bunker—I wasn't kidding. Weapons. Research. Supplies. Enough to survive pretty much anything."

Inara's eyes widen. "Cian, that's a lot. I can't believe your aunt was really your mom. And I have to see this basement."

She rubs my back gently, grounding me. I don't mention the world-ending gem yet. One apocalypse at a time. Out of nowhere, she slugs me in the arm. Hard.

"If you ever lie to me again," she warns.

"I'll give you a reason to steal one of my lives. Got it?"

I laugh and nod. She kisses me. With that adorable threat, I realize something's cracked open in me. I'd built up walls so high, but she found a way in. I don't yet know how to let her stay... but I know I am not going to let her go.

"You're the most beautiful, most frustrating woman I've ever met," I say.

"I crave you. And I can't stand the thought of being away from you again. I'll never lie to you. I swear it. As long as you'll have me, I'm yours."

I take her face in my hands and kiss her forehead. Her cheeks flush, and I see it...nervous excitement. Her lip catches between her teeth and my focus sharpens. She squirms under my gaze like prey. I feel wild, possessive even, as I prowl forward and wrap my arm around her waist. Her breath deepens. My hand finds her curves, and my lips hover just above her neck.

"Cian. Please... please kiss me," she whispers so soft I barely catch it.

That's all I need. I kiss and bite her neck, hard and hungry. I lift her into my arms and lay her on the nearest surface. I unzip her dress, pulling it down to reveal her perfect curves wrapped in lace again. I'll tease her later for wearing something so damn sexy during the apocalypse. My lips find her breast, her soft moans driving me to the edge. I kiss every inch of her body making her back arche, and she begs me, breathless.

"I need you. All of you," she says.

I press between her thighs giving her exactly what she needs. Her hands tangle in my hair, her legs locking around me until her body quivers with release.

She's breathtaking…flushed, smiling, radiant. I kiss her slowly, savoring every second.

"You're mine," I whisper.

"And I'm never losing you again."

She opens her mouth to say something, but I stop her with another kiss, taking her face in my hands. Some things don't need words. Suddenly, the moment is interrupted by emergency sirens outside. We're snapped back to reality. The world might be ending out there but part of me thinks that's exactly why we should keep going.

"The world is facing impending doom. We should probably figure out how to stop it and find our friends," Inara says with a smirk, though she's just as disappointed as I am that we were interrupted.

Remembering why she came over in the first place, I spring back and offer her a hand off the counter. The world is drowning in darkness, slipping into chaos, and we're no closer to a solution. I can't stop thinking about how good she tastes or how badly I want to continue what we started, but the seriousness of the situation outside tugs at my attention again as the echo of a loud crash, followed by distant screams makes me on edge.

"Inara... I'm the cause of this. If I hadn't used my abilities to steal that life, none of this would've happened. I upset Fate, whatever that is." I say, staring out the window at the chaos I unleashed.

Inara adjusts her black skirt, smirking like she knows something I don't.

"How could you be the cause? Do you control the weather now? Does Abacus? Actually, he might. But seriously, you took one life and left that waiter with the rest of his beads. It was an accident. Clare took a life too and the world didn't end. You can't carry this blame. You have to forgive yourself," she says, rubbing my back gently, her logic grounding me.

"Okay, fair... but I did something that felt sinister, and it was powerful enough to change my eye color. We have no idea what stealing a life really does. Clare wrote about the darkness building inside until we're nothing but husks. I don't want to become that," I mutter, hanging my head low.

"That's right—I almost forgot Clare was actually your mom. This is a lot. How are you holding up?" Inara asks, her voice soft with concern.

"It is a lot. but I think deep down I always knew. I just wish I could see her one more time. Still, at least I know the truth now," I say, still wishing I knew more about my father.

"I always felt guilty loving my aunt more than my parents but turns out, my heart knew the truth all along. It's actually kind of a relief," I add, pulling her into a hug.

"Come on, let's assess the situation outside, and try to find a way to fix this," I say, pointing us toward the door.

I follow her out, and we're immediately greeted by a street clogged with abandoned vehicles. Police cruisers and ambulances are still lit up, sirens blaring, but there's no one inside. Trees burn from lightning strikes, and we hear screaming in the distance, hidden by smoke and haze.

"Where are all the drivers?" Inara asks, her voice tight.

"Don't look," I say, turning her into my chest to shield her from what's ahead.

But it's too late. The vehicles aren't abandoned—just filled with drivers who no longer breathe. I try to keep Inara from seeing, but she pulls away, only to find the horror waiting for her.

"What could've done this to them?" she cries.

"We'll find out. The news said people were trying to flee the city, but they had to shut down highways. There just weren't enough resources to respond to the accidents," I say, pulling her back into my arms.

If I'm not the cause of this, then what is? What made Abacus reap so many lives? It had to be him, right? The question haunts me as we rush back inside and head straight for the basement. I remember him asking for my help but what could death possibly need me for?

"This is the safest place for now. Maybe Clare left something in her research that can help," I say, grabbing Spencer and leading us downstairs.

...

Hours pass. We're no closer to stopping this apocalypse.

"What if this really is Abacus?" Inara asks.

"Did you find something?" I ask, moving to where she's clutching a folder from the box labeled Out of Time.

"Clare's notes mention a similar storm in the 1700s. Same lightning, no rain. People dropping dead from unknown causes. Apparently, something upset the natural order. Sound familiar?" Her nose scrunches when she's excited, and I fall under her spell again as she looks up at me with those gorgeous green eyes.

"It says Death was the cause of it and was on a rampage for an unknown reason." Inara continues.

"Then we can be certain Abacus is the cause of this. Now how do we stop him before the whole world is destroyed?" I ask.

Then I remember what Abacus's is after.

"Inara, I never finished telling you what Abacus wanted. I forgot with everything else that happened. He wants to be mortal again," I say, handing her the box that Clare left for me.

"Inside is a map to a gem that might be powerful enough to stop Abacus or give him exactly what he wants. Clare said it has the power to resurrect a life but for a cost. Abacus wants to be mortal again and I think he could use this gem to do just that which is why she said we had to protect the knowledge of the gem at all costs. If it's that powerful, I wonder if it could somehow be used to defeat him or restore the natural order. It's from the original Death's abacus."

"I'm too young and fashionable to be dealing with an apocalypse" she mutters. I laugh, pull her into my arms and kiss the top of her head, trying to comfort her as an expression of resignation washes over her face.

"So, we use the map to find the gem and stop Abacus?"

"Maybe we could use it to lure him into a trap... though, can you even kill Death? Would the world survive without him maintaining the balance?"

"I don't know, Cian. I can't even move when Abacus is around, the way you can. None of us can. This sounds dangerous and I don't even know how we can help you. Even still I wish Vale, Charlie, and John were here."

"I'm sorry. I never meant to drag you into this but you have to admit we make a great team gorgeous. Just knowing you are with me gives me the strength to face this."

"Cian, if it's the end of the world, then the only place I want to be is by your side," she says with a small smile.

For the first time in a very long time, I have someone to protect and I'll be damned if I let anything hurt her. The stakes are high. One wrong move and we lose everything. We're up against Abacus. A chill runs down my spine. I feel something pulling at me, warning me of what's to come.

"I want to try something," I say, standing with purpose.

"I'm going to drop my shield and try to find Abacus. Maybe I can reason with him or at least gather information."

"I don't like this plan," she says, voice shaking.

"What if he takes all your lives?"

"Inara, I have to try. Trust me."

"Cian, this is insane. He's death."

"Do you trust me?" I say.

"I trust you. But this is risky. What if I lose you?"

"You can't get rid of me that easy, sweetheart." I kiss her forehead.

"You better not die, or I'll kill you," she whispers.

I laugh, surprised and maybe a little terrified by her words. My sweet, stubborn girl. I kiss her deeply. It nearly changes my mind, but the pull is back. I have to go.

"I'll always come back to you, Inara."

"Remember, this is just recon. Come back in one piece." she says.

"You stay here. Keep reading. Maybe you can decipher the map in case we do need it. If anyone can, it's you."

I don't say I love you, but I feel it as I head for the door. I walk several blocks before dropping my shield, just in case this crazy plan works.

The streets are dark and deserted. My new powers are still unpredictable, and Abacus could be anywhere. Clare said his realm exists beyond time... maybe that's how he's everywhere at once.

"This should be far enough," I mutter, letting my shield drop.

I feel lighter and more capable with my shield down. I walk a few more blocks, but see no one. I change tactics, heading toward Wrigley. If anywhere still has life, it's there—drunken chaos or riots, maybe both. The neon Cubs sign glows ahead, giving me hope. Maybe someone's still out there. Rain pours out of nowhere. Normally, I love the rain, but not today. Not when it's soaking through my clothes and slowing me down. Admitting defeat, I duck into a bar. As I open the door, the rain stops... and a chill runs up my spine. Abacus is here. I smirk—my plan worked. But I didn't think past this moment. What now?

"Maybe this time it will work," I hear from across the room.

Pain stabs through my chest. This is bad. Abacus has two men and a woman frozen, three beads on his ring. He starts removing them one by one. As each vanishes, their bodies fall to the floor.

"What have you done?" I shout, stepping from the shadows.

He crosses the hundred-foot distance in a blink.

"Now, Cian, is that any way to speak to your superior?" he says.

"Have you thought more about my offer?

"I wouldn't have done this if you'd helped. Every life I've taken is on your shoulders. So... will you help me become mortal, or shall I start killing everyone you love? Starting with, Inara, was it?"

"Don't you dare touch her. She has nothing to do with this. It's me you want!" I yell, heart pounding.

But I'm frozen, waist-deep in invisible tar. I can't move. He's trapping me with his power. Why did I think this was a good idea? Abacus has me right where he wants me. Way to go Marine, rushing into the fire without a second thought.

He's leaving me no choice but to consider bluffing my way out of this mess. I think back to playing poker with Clare and what she taught me about bluffing your opponent. Don't let them see your emotions. Her first rule—for poker, for lying, and for life.

"Abacus, you win. I should have helped you. I'll tell you everything I know," I say as calmly as possible, trying not to raise his suspicions.

"Share all your knowledge with me, boy," Abacus demands, placing his hand on my head.

What's happening to me? I feel him rifling through my memories, tearing through my mind. I have to fight back, fast, before he finds it. My eyes dart across the bar, searching for weapons, exits, anything I can use to distract him. Maybe there's a gun behind the bar. Not that it would help. He's already dead—that's kind of his whole thing.

Then I hear Clare's voice in my mind, whispering one word: *"Shield."*

Of course. My shield. I center myself and focus everything I have, pulling my shield back up and locking it in place like a vault.

"I changed my mind. I'm not helping you!" I say sharply, breaking free from his mental grip.

I stumble a few steps toward the door but he's already there, materializing in front of me before I can make it away.

"Enough wasting my time," he growls.

"What do you know that can give me life again? I know there has to be a way. I've seen the research your mother left behind. Clare made you promise to protect something very powerful. If it's that important, then maybe that's what I need."

He raises the golden abacus in his hand and calls forth one of my beads.

"I'll tell you everything I know but only if you fix the sky. Stop the storms and killing," I say, trying to barter with death like he's some used car salesman.

"Do not push me, boy," he snarls.

"I have no patience for insolence. And I haven't set fire to your realm—yet. I could stop reaping... but only after you make me mortal. Only then can I return to my family and you can have your peace."

He squeezes one of my beads tightly between his fingers, and I feel my chest seize.

"Now, tell me where to find this object!"

I'm out of options. Letting him dig through my memories again is a worse alternative. So, I trust my gut and go with it.

"There may be a way to resurrect you," I say, carefully choosing my words.

"All I know is that it's an ancient and powerful gem, rumored to restore the life of anyone."

I leave out the map. I leave out Inara. He doesn't need to know everything. Maybe giving him this much will be enough to make him stop killing, to restore some kind of balance.

"If you give me the gem," Abacus says slowly,

"I will stop reaping everyone. I'll let you and your loved ones live. You have my word."

He gestures over his chest like he's swearing on a heart…if he even has one. I'm caught off guard. His offer could save countless lives. If he really was mortal once, maybe there is a way to bring him back. This is all so far above my head, and none of it makes sense. But Clare warned me. Never let the gem fall into the wrong hands. And Abacus is the definition of the wrong hands.

"Will you help me, Cian?" he asks.

"I had a family, just like you. I gave up my life to save them and I was cursed for it."

For a moment, he almost sounds human. I feel that same pull…deep, heavy, undeniable. And before I can stop myself, the secret slips out.

"I have a map to the gem that can resurrect the dead. It's stored in my basement. Wait—no! I didn't mean to say that," I blurt, trying to pull the words back, but it's too late.

Shame floods me instantly. Clare warned me this knowledge was dangerous. And I just handed it over like a rookie. What the hell is wrong with me? Abacus smiles. A satisfied, bone-deep grin. Before I can move, before I can even think, his hand clamps down on my shoulder and the world blinks out.

"Good boy." He says with that arrogant tone.

CHAPTER 14
CIAN: UNHINGED

In an instant, I recognize we're back in my living room, Abacus's grip on my shoulder still firm, unrelenting. His effortless ability to transport us leaves me both awed and unnerved, wondering what else he's capable of. I am completely outmatched.

"Make haste, time in this realm eludes me. Fetch the map swiftly and deliver it to me. I will not ask again," Abacus commands, effortlessly propelling me forward.

Dread surges through me as I remember—Inara is still here. She's now in the most dangerous place on earth because of me. Panic grips my chest. I tremble at the thought of Abacus realizing I can't decipher the map or confirm if the gem even exists. I need to buy time… and keep him away from her. Maybe he's limited somehow, tied to his realm, unable to linger long. A flicker of hope.

"Abacus, the truth is…the gem isn't here. In fact, I'm not even sure it exists. I just need a few days. I'm close. I can find something," I say, mixing just enough truth with the lie to make it believable.

"Do you think I'm that easy to deceive? We're here because you brought us. This is where you hid the map. Do not play games with me. Bring me my map!" Abacus flexes his power, reminding me how insignificant I am compared to him.

"I swear, I'm not lying. I have old drawings, maybe a map, but I can't decipher it yet. With the chaos you've caused, no one could. If you halt the storms, restore some order, then maybe I can help."

"Interesting," he muses, then narrows his eyes.

"Why are you so desperate to keep me from the basement? Is it the girl?" A grin creeps across his face.

"Ah, a wonderful idea. Let us say hello. It may motivate you."

"No, wait! I'll get the map. Just wait here." I bolt toward the basement door, praying he doesn't follow.

"I may have been born at night, but not last night." Before I can blink, he teleports us both into the basement.

"There she is." he says staring at her frozen in place.

"If you touch one hair on her head, I'll end you—immortal or not!" I growl.

"Fetch my map, boy," he says, ignoring my threat completely.

It stings more than I expect—that he didn't even dignify it with a response. He knows he holds all the power. But maybe… maybe this sword Clare left behind will change that.

"Coming right up," I mutter, pointing to the table the chest is on and moving as quickly as possible, hoping he doesn't sense my real plan.

I reach down and wrap my fingers around the sword's leather handle. Power surges through me like electricity, flooding every nerve with strength. Confidence. I swing the blue-glowing blade at Abacus's head with everything I've got.

The gem in the hilt shines so bright it blinds us both. A jolt of energy rockets through my arms as I hit something hard...something that stops the blade cold. I close my eyes and try again, but a burst of light explodes from the blade, knocking me back with a shockwave. I can't tell if I struck him or the wall, but I prepare myself for whatever comes next.

As the light fades and my vision returns, I see the golden abacus arcing toward my head. I raise the sword just in time to block. The sound of metal and magic colliding echoes through the room. I'm literally fighting Death. We lock eyes and then suddenly, he vanishes. The room goes still. Normal. My heart is pounding. I spin and find her.

"Inara, are you okay?" I drop the sword and rush to her, pulling her into my arms.

"Cian? I didn't even hear you come back. What's with the sword?" Her voice is confused, breathless, full of questions I can't yet answer.

I just hold her. As long as she'll let me. Minutes pass before she gently pulls back, eyes searching mine. Then she kisses me, soft and sincere.

"Can you tell me what happened now?"

"I thought I was going to lose you," I say, voice hoarse.

"Abacus found me. He forced me to bring him here."

"I have so many questions," she says, gently touching my cheek.

"I found him after searching for hours. He took the lives of three people before I even got close. I failed. Worse, I brought him here, within inches of you. He wants to be mortal again, and he'll burn the world to do it."

"Promise me," she says, her voice trembling.

"Anything." I answer.

"Never leave me behind again."

"Never again," I vow, without hesitation.

"Besides, you're way too intelligent to bench. I am certain if you had these powers Abacus would already be defeated."

She punches my shoulder with a teasing jab, laughter bubbling up, and I know I scared her more than she's letting on. If that sword hadn't worked—

"Wait. You used that sword against Abacus and lived?" she says, realization dawning.

"What is it made of?" she asks

"I don't know. But it worked. It bought us time." I grip her hand.

"He'll be back soon. We need to prepare."

"We're not safe here," I add, pressing a kiss to her forehead.

"And I noticed something…Abacus looked the same again. He's not changing anymore."

"I think that's what he looked like when he was mortal. It must be connected to why he's acting different."

I toss some weapons and supplies into a bag. We head upstairs. The sky is still dark and violent. Abacus is still out there, stealing lives and chasing the one thing he thinks can save him. I look at Inara and notice she's shaking so I wrap my arm around her. And suddenly, all I can think about is how close I came to losing her. The world is falling apart, death is hunting us, but in this moment holding her I realize life is too short to waste a second.

"It's just you and me. I wish we could just run away together. Escape all of this." I whisper.

"That sounds perfect," she sighs,

"But we're probably the only ones who can stop him. The sword must be the way to do it. Otherwise, he wouldn't have blocked it. After we save the world, though? Italy. Or Paris."

I chuckle and pull her close again and kiss her. She is everything I want. Everything I can't lose. The weight of the world vanishes under her touch.

"I love you, Cian," she says, so softly I almost miss it.

"I love you too," I whisper back.

"Sweetheart, I have to stop Abacus. Keeping you safe is everything. I'll find him again and use this sword to finish this fight. You need to go somewhere else to keep the map hidden, even from me. If he reads my mind again—"

"Cian this is madness; how would you even find me after? And you just promised you wouldn't do this!" she says with anger building in her voice.

"I'll always find you gorgeous." I say trying to be charming, hoping to diffuse her anger.

"What if you don't?" she says with fear written all over her face.

"Then you find the gem on the map and use it to kill Abacus." I say and brush her hair from her face as gently as I can.

"We need to warn the others. This plan doesn't make sense." Inara quips.

"Backup could be helpful I suppose, but I would rather keep all of you safe and that means far away from me." I say and reach for her shoulders this time, but she tosses my hands away.

"Are you kidding me? After everything, you're going to run off alone, again?" she says with steam practically coming out of her ears.

Her anger is electric and God help me; I'm turned on by it.

"Inara, I promise this is the last time. It's important that you go hide the map while I do this. I'll drop my shield, bait Abacus into coming back, and end this." I insist.

I step in to comfort her, but the second I try she shoves me away again.

"Cian... stop trying to pacify me!" she yells.

"Inara, we have to stop Abacus and I'm the only one of us who can move when he is near," I say, the words solidifying in my chest with painful clarity.

This is my fault and I have to fix it... alone. The sun refuses to rise, just as it has since Abacus unleashed his chaos on the world, leaving everything in shadows.

"I don't like the idea of you facing him alone again. He is Death, after all, and who knows what else he is capable of. Please change your mind and let me come with you," Inara pleads, looking up at me with those emerald green eyes.

All I see is a damsel I have to protect at any cost, even though I know she's strong and capable in her own right. It's not fair to her, but I'd rather die right now than allow her to be harmed in any way. She's right, this plan isn't great but I'm not about to admit that to her and there's no way I can let her come with me to face certain death. Even if I find Abacus again and manage to stop him with the sword, I'm pretty sure I won't make it out alive. This is a one-way mission. I have the sword and a gut feeling that I can actually stop him with it. It's like Clare is telling me herself, *you can do this.* A warm, comforting wave washes over me.

"He's probably coming back for the map any minute. We've already stayed here longer than we should have. I don't regret a single minute with you, sweetheart, but I need you to take the map, leave, and don't tell me where you're going. Try to figure out where the map leads to if you can, and keep trying to connect with the group," I say, grabbing something to eat from the fridge before we part ways.

"Okay, fine. I'll go." She signs throwing her hands up in resignation.

"But what's your plan this time?" she asks.

"Don't worry. I'm a Marine, remember? I got this. The plan is foolproof," I say with a confident smile, trying to charm my way back into her good graces.

"So… no plan yet," she laughs breaking the tension.

I nod. I have no idea what my next move is, but I have to try. If I run, he'll just find us anyway. The sword seems strong enough to at least defend against him, but I'm betting it can hurt him too. I just need to get him distracted long enough to drop his guard.

"I'll drop my shield again to find him, but this time I have the sword and what he wants most... a map. Or at least that's what I plan to let him believe." I add, trying to sound like I've got more than half a plan.

"You promise to come back to me?" Inara asks as a tear rolls down her cheek.

"I promise. I'll always come back to you, sweetheart. Be safe out there and don't forget to take Spencer with you," I say, kissing her forehead, bending to pat him on the head, and picking up my sword.

We leave in opposite directions—one to find Abacus, the other to attempt to decipher the map from a safe location. I let my feelings guide me and start dropping my shield the moment Inara is out of sight. The streets are full of wrecked cars, and it's obvious the power is out on the whole block. The sky looks like it's splitting apart, violet lightning flashing nonstop. It's a ghost town out here. At least this time, I know there won't be innocent bystanders when I face Abacus.

...

Several hours of wandering the city with my shield down, and I somehow end up at the Lincoln Park Zoo. I love this place. It was my favorite as a kid. I've been all around the world, but this zoo still holds a special place in my heart. Whatever Abacus is up to, I'm not having any luck finding him. Might as well see if I can get in. The gates are wide open and no staff in sight, which is weird.

"Where are all the animals?" I say aloud, standing in the middle of an empty zoo that once brought me so much joy, but now just reminds me how desperate things have gotten.

...

Defeated, I make my way home. The silence and her absence hang in the air like a heavy weight pressing down on my chest. Inara's warm welcome has quickly become something I count on, and now, thanks to me, it's gone. I can only hope she's faring better than I am.

I sigh and head for the shower, hoping the water can wash away the exhaustion that clings to me, weighing me down. The hot stream pours over me, unwinding the tension in my muscles, the tightness I hadn't even realized I'd been carrying.

I step out of the shower and into my bedroom, collapsing onto the bed, allowing myself a moment of stillness. Just a moment to breathe. I allow my thoughts to drift back to Inara and our time together. But then, it hits me. A cold shiver crawls down my spine, despite the warmth surrounding me.

"Abacus," I whisper, the word escaping my lips like a breath of dread.

He's here. And before I can get up, he appears in my room just a few feet away.

"I'm here for the map, boy. Don't play games with me again, or you will die. And so will the girl," Abacus growls.

"Wait… are you naked?" he adds, with a hint of surprise in that ominous tone, clearly not intending to catch me in the buff.

"I'm surprised nakedness offends you, considering how casually you murder people. But yes, I was relaxing when you decided to crash the party. Maybe we can reschedule for tomorrow?" I reply, sarcasm in my voice.

I grab a towel and wrap it around myself, trying to plan my next move. I swear I see a smirk tug at his grim face, but it fades fast. He steps back, letting me walk into my closet to get dressed.

Before I can finish pulling my shirt on, he demands again.

"Give me the map. Now!"

"No need to get worked up. I've got it gift-wrapped for you. I hid it to keep it safe. Didn't want you to spoil Christmas," I say, heading downstairs to the front closet.

"You're taking too long. I'm almost out of time. Hurry up!" he snaps, suddenly appearing behind me.

Creepy as hell.

"Hold your horses," I say opening the hall closet.

"I've got what you want right here." And then I turn and swing the sword at him in a blur of blue steel.

The blade hits tile. He's gone. I search the house frantically, heart pounding, trying to make sure he's not about to ambush me. He only needs one strike to end me.

"Abacus? Where'd you go, pal?"

My mind jumps to Inara to what he might do if he realizes she has the map. I grab my keys, sword in hand, and race to my car. I have to reach her first. The streets are a mess of wreckage, but I swerve and speed around the chaos. I try calling…nothing. Lines are dead. Power's still out. I get as close to her apartment as I can before barricades block every street. She has to be there.

"Guess I'm walking the rest of the way," I mutter, grabbing the sword and running.

If anyone saw me right now, they'd either think I'm a badass out to slay a monster… or a lunatic who escaped from a hospital. Just a few more blocks. Come on, Marine. A blue light flashes in the corner of my eye as I run down the deserted street. I don't have time for the Police today. Inara needs me. Stay on mission. She's strong. She'll be okay.

CHAPTER 15
ABACUS: NO WAY OUT

He thinks he's clever—thinks he can catch me off guard. Fool. He has no idea who he's dealing with. Nothing and no one will stop me from obtaining the gem. It's my key to life and to reuniting with my family. First, I will become mortal and then I will resurrect them all. I will see you soon my love.

"You're taking too long; the void is already starting to pull me back. Hurry up!" I demand.

I need to make him drop his guard, to open his mind just enough for me to slip inside. But as I look at him, I realize he no longer has the map. Instead, he charges at me again, sword raised. Laughable. As if this mortal could ever harm me. Nothing can kill me and that's the problem. The girl. Inara. She must have it. The Void tugs at me again, pulling me closer. My time is almost up.

Cian steps forward, reckless as ever, his resolve burning through the tension in the air. But before I can end his insufferable defiance, I'm pulled back. Swallowed by the Void once more. I've managed to stretch the time between returns by channeling the lives I collect, but it's not enough anymore. The pressure to complete the list is maddening. It takes everything I have to keep it from devouring my mind. The longer I ignore it, the more names appear.

Every time I reset in the Void, it pulls me toward the next one. But still, I grow stronger with every life I claim from the ring. Map or not, I will get what I want…one way or another. The ring gleams in my grip, its power guiding me toward the next soul: Jennifer Ruth, Gary, Indiana. How bleak.

I'm running on pure instinct now, no thought or hesitation. I take all her lives in an instant, the soul slipping from her as easily as the flick of a switch. And then, I'm back in the Void.

"Hahaha!"

Was that me? The laughter feels foreign, almost detached. Am I losing myself to this hunger... this insatiable lust for life?

That feeling again, the sensation of being watched. Impossible. There's no one here. Just the doomed, the discarded souls that hold no weight, no meaning. Once I return to the mortal realm, they won't matter. Not anymore. They'll serve me—my army of lost souls. Perhaps I could use them to reshape the world in my image.

The thought stirs something deep inside me, something cold and burning. A fire in my chest. If I still had a chest. If I still had blood to pump.

"Are you entertained?" I shout into the endless black of the void.

"I know someone's there. Show yourself!"

Silence. Maybe I am alone, or maybe I'm just slipping further into madness. To dull the ache of it, I start reaping names again. Five lives from a man in Beijing, dust in my hands. A couple in New York, gone just as quickly. On and on, I collect soul after soul, until the weight of my mission fades into the rush of power that surges through me.

I need more lives—more souls—to harness their power, to restore my lifeline. The beads aren't disintegrating as fast anymore, which might mean I simply need more of them. Maybe then I will be able to hold on to the lives long enough to place them on the ring to give me a lifeline again. Only then will I be able to regain what I've lost.

Still, I feel... more. Every life I take gives me something. A whisper of sensation. A shred of memory. At this rate, I wonder if I'll have to reap the entire world to become alive again. But I'll do it. My family's faces play on a loop in my mind. I hear my little girl's voice crying out for me.

"I'm coming home."

...

I leave a trail of bodies across the world. Their souls trapped in the Void, unable to rest until I do. Fate has bound them to me. If I stay, so do they. But when I rise, they'll rise too and remain loyal to me. When I reclaim my humanity, they'll serve a greater purpose.

I decide I need a crowd, somewhere dense with souls. More than one life at a time. As if answering me, the ring transports us. A wedding. The bride and groom stand frozen just feet from me. Joy painted across their faces. She wears white satin, delicate lace, so familiar. I remember my own wedding. My wife's smile. For a moment, I feel peace. Real peace. The first in centuries. But it fades. The pull of the Void returns. Duty over desire.

"Congratulations," I whisper to the frozen bride as I pass, heading toward the man choking on his dinner.

His name is on my list. I don't remember love. Not really. But something inside me still wants it. Craves it. So, I leave the others untouched…for now. I take only the life that's owed and vanish. Back in the Void again. Surrounded by lost souls, drifting. Shredding the last remnants of who they were before I liberated them. Soon, they'll become something more, useful.

I've lost focus, but no more. I need that map. Cian is the key. I can feel it. Our fate is connected and once I have that gem, I know I can use it to live once more since all other plans continue to fail me.

"I'm done with your list!" I shout into the Void.

Then I'm gone. I teleport across the world, hunting dense pockets of souls. In England, I take twenty. In Germany, fifty. In India, a thousand souls fall in one sweep, and the only change. A tingle in my hand. A reddish flicker before it all turns to ash. Still not enough. The Void drags me back. I stay only as long as I must, then continue the harvest. Thousands fall. Still nothing. I need that gem. The one Cian promised. As I ponder my next move, the ring teleports us.

"Why this place?" I ask, as if the ring could answer.

My mind works fast to solve the puzzle. Cian. The map. He tried to trick me but now I remember Inara, she has it.

...

"Remember me?" I ask, voice low and cold.

"Abacus!" She gasps, horrified.

She's clearly not special.

"I'll make you a deal," I say smoothly.

"Tell me where the map is, and I'll let you live."

"I don't know where it is," she lies.

Obvious. Desperate.

"I'm tired of your lies." I pluck a bead from her lifeline. Slowly. It turns a vibrant red before vanishing.

"Tick tock. You don't have many lives left, deary. What will it be?" I say, taking more, until only one remains.

"I know you have it. Just tell me where you hid it. I'll leave you with one life so you can watch me cleanse this world when I break free of this prison."

She trembles. "Do you promise not to hurt Cian if I give you the map?"

"This deal saves you. He sealed his fate long ago." I step toward her and release my grip on her movements so she may retrieve my map.

"Go! Fetch my map and you shall live, brief though your remaining time may be."

She stands there looking at me in shock.

"Hurry up!" I bark.

"Why... why can I move?" she stammers.

"No questions! Just get it!"

"Okay, okay! I hid it in the back closet," she says, running down the hall.

While she searches, I examine the tiny frozen creature in the living room. A dog. But so small clearly not purebred. No use in battle. No defense from raiders. Not like the beasts I once knew.

"Hurry up, girl or you will die!" I raise the ring, her last bead between my fingers...

She marches in, sees me looking at her dog.

"Hurt him and I'll kill you." She yells.

"Boom!"

The door explodes. I feel the Void pulling again.

"Inara, are you here?" Cian's voice.

"Cian, run! Abacus is here!" She shouts and lunges at me with a kitchen knife.

"Bollocks!"

Before I can retaliate, the Void rips me back like a rubber band. So close. Again. Next time, I will kill them both straight away. Maybe the dog can fetch the map from their corpses. The darkness mutes everything here. The whispers of the lost souls grow louder. Restless.

I'm exhausted by being so close, yet so far. I need that gem. Or maybe... maybe I just need the right leverage. Cian cares for her. He's tried to save her more than once. Perhaps she's the key. Once I take her final life, he'll have no choice but to find the gem to bring her back. And when he does, I'll be there, waiting to take it for myself. I will use the gem to save myself, to find my family. And then, I'll be free. Free from this endless cycle, free from the Void. Finally, everything will be mine.

CHAPTER 16
CIAN: THE DARKNESS

I kick in the door easily and watch as it breaks apart, flying into the apartment. I can't make out what she's saying, but I know that voice. It's her. I run inside and find Inara and Spencer in the living room, alone, to my surprise.

"Was Abacus here?" I ask, stunned to find them unharmed.

"He was," she replies, her voice steady despite the chaos.

"He took all but my last life to get the map, but I didn't give in. I knew you'd never break, so I didn't either." She gestures with the kitchen knife in her hand, a quiet strength in her movement.

"You tried to stab Abacus with a kitchen knife?" I ask, my disbelief mixing with admiration.

"I'm so sorry I let this happen," I say, guilt weighing on my words.

"I never should've put you in harm's way." Carefully, I grasp her knife-holding hand and ease the blade from her fingers, just in case Abacus tries to summon himself again.

"I figured it was better than just letting him take my last life, you know?" She shrugs with a sad smile.

"You may look innocent and harmless, but underneath it all, you're a warrior." I wrap an arm around her waist and kiss her forehead.

Spencer nudges my leg with his nose, demanding attention. I pat his head but keep my grip on Inara. This burden is mine to bear. I should never have left her to protect the map; she could have died and now she only has one life left thanks to me. Abacus's rampage began with my reckless decision to save myself, followed by my betrayal of Clare, revealing to him the one thing I should've kept buried forever.

Now, he's hunting us for the map, desperate to gain ultimate power that could very well destroy all life as we know it. This… this is all on me.

As if she can read my thoughts she says,

"Cian, this isn't all your fault. Sure, I might've been safer if I hadn't taken the map, but then you would've been in danger too."

She kisses my cheek with such gentle understanding that it takes me by surprise, as if she somehow knows I'm lost in my own doubts, that I need her love to pull myself back. I don't deserve her, and a nagging fear creeps in…that maybe, just maybe, I really am the monster I've always feared I could become.

"Abacus came after me too. That's how I knew to come here. When he vanished, I figured he'd head for you, but I don't get why he left without finishing things. Something else is going on," I say, not letting her out of my arms.

"We've tried countless times to stop him, and we're no better off than when we started. It's like we can't win, Cian!" Inara says, stepping back, her voice breaking with defeat as she crumbles under the weight of it all.

"Where's the map?"

"There's a hidden compartment in my closet; I usually store my passport and stuff in there. I put it inside," she says, leading me into her bedroom.

"We have to destroy it," I say, my stomach tightening.

"Cian, if we do that, no one will ever find the gem. What if it's the only way to stop Abacus?" she asks, handing me the map reluctantly.

"Even so, it's too much power for anyone to have. If it's between Abacus getting it or no one, the only smart option is no one. He's already close to ending everything without it." I take the map and head for the door.

Outside, I find a metal trash can and use the lighter I borrowed from Inara to burn the map and the gem drawings. The fire's glow reminds me of San Diego evenings during my time in the Marines—the ocean waves crashing, the sun sinking behind the water. The red and yellow flames dance through my mind as the map to the gem turns to ash.

For a moment, I thought about using it to bring Clare back, but I know that's not what she would want. Noone should have this much power. I glance up at the cursed sky, then at my watch. It should be sunny and 75, but we're stuck in this endless night that's destroying everything. If we don't stop him soon, it'll be too late.

"Fuck!" I yell startling Inara.

I take a deep breath. *Breathe, Cian. Get it together.* As we step inside, Inara breaks down, her walls crumbling as the weight of everything hits her.

"Cian, I don't know what to do. I'm terrified. Abacus could return at any moment and I'll be frozen again, powerless to stop him from taking my last life," Inara says, her voice trembling with a mix of terror and fury.

"I promise I'll protect you," I whisper, pulling her close.

But the words hang in the air, fragile and hollow, because the truth is, I have little power to control any of this.

"Sweetheart, we'll find a way together this time," I say, offering her a soft smile meant to ease her fears, though inside, there's no relief.

Clare's journal spoke of balance as the key to mastering this curse. But I've been anything but balanced. Her words suddenly echo in my mind.

"When the soul drifts askew, shadows gather and the vale thins—those we love stand to bleed first."

I feel a sudden all-consuming anger building within me. Abacus is unhinged and will destroy us all in his quest to become mortal, but he fails to understand that I will sacrifice the world to save Inara. Let it burn! What's the world ever done for me anyways.

Something inside me is breaking, slowly, piece by piece. And for the first time, I'm starting to embrace it. Drunk on the power, the freedom, as rage takes hold and consumes me.

"You, okay? You've been quiet," Inara asks gently.

"Never better, sweetheart," I say with a smile.

"I'm going to end Abacus," I add, dead set on gaining the strength to stop him.

He'll be back for the map soon and I will enjoy the moment he realizes that I took this from him.

"Cian, did you see John's email?" Inara says pulling me back to the present.

"No, what's going on?"

"He says the storms are all connected."

I can't believe it; we finally got a response. Thank God John's still alive.

"We already knew they're caused by the natural order being upset," I say.

"No, Cian! Look. They're literally connected. One massive storm, covering the entire planet," she says, showing me the apocalyptic satellite image.

"We'll stop this before the world ends," I say, my voice steady, trying to reassure her, even as my anger fuels the growing desire to end Abacus once and for all.

"Let's head back to my place. Message John to gather the others and meet us there. We need their help to come up with a plan that might actually work. I think we're running out of chances so we have to get this right." I say, pulling her close for a kiss before she can respond.

"You seem off, Cian." Inara says with Spencer in tow as she opens the door.

"Are you sure you're, okay?" Inara asks.

"I'm great, just ready to end this sweetheart." I say but see the skepticism in her eyes.

She reaches for my hand as we step outside. Just her touch grounds me and steadies my thoughts. It reminds me of the future I hope to have with her once all of this madness is no longer consuming our lives.

The sound of alarms ringing nearby interrupts my peaceful thoughts bringing me back to the present. Suddenly I hear a woman's scream and my heart sinks as Inara abruptly pulls her hand free from mine while yelling that we have to help and bolts toward the chaos. If I weren't so damn frightened for her, I'd be impressed. Afterall, Marines run toward danger. They don't retreat.

"Inara, stop!" I shout, chasing after her.

I scoop up Spencer and sprint after her, every possible nightmare I can imagine flooding my mind. I round the corner and find the reality of the situation playing out exactly as I feared—Inara standing alone in front of four men, all armed with makeshift weapons. The city is a war zone, the police nowhere to be found. We're on our own.

"Look, gentlemen, we're just passing through. We don't want trouble, and we'll be on our way." I keep my voice steady as I place Spencer down and slowly position myself between Inara and the men, shielding her body with mine. As their attention shifts, I see the woman they were harassing swiftly flee down the street to safety. At least this disaster wasn't entirely pointless, I think to myself.

"Don't leave just yet, pretty girl," the man I now refer to as Dead Man Walking #1 says, bouncing a metal pipe in his hands as they begin to circle us. "We all might die tomorrow, and I can think of plenty of fun things to do with you before then."

My blood boils. I can't believe what these animals are implying. "I don't think you heard me. We're leaving now. Move, or it won't end well for you."

"That's not very nice," Dead Man #2 sneers. "We just want to have a little fun before the end."

Spencer starts growling and barking right as Dead Man #2 swings the bat, and I take it in the shoulder, my teeth gritting against the pain. I counter with a kick to his chest that sends him sprawling to the ground. He'll be back up soon, but I don't have time for him. Inara's in danger, and I need to get her to safety.

"You're going to pay for that, asshole," Dead Man #3 says, eyeing Inara like she's prey. The sick smile on his face makes my blood run cold. My anger is starting to boil over so I focus on the pain in my shoulder to ground myself before I do something reckless, like end all of them right now. I know they'll kill us both if they get the chance so why should I care about their lives.

"I'll kill all of you if you even look at her again!" I growl, narrowing my eyes, scanning their every move trying to keep her behind me.

"She is going to taste really sweet once I have her on her back" REALLY FUCKING Dead Man #4 says, walking up to us without fear. A mistake. And I plan to take advantage of it.

Before I can react, Inara steps in front of me, her fist connecting with his face in a perfect, jaw-rattling punch. He drops like a sack of bricks, and my chest tightens with admiration as I pull her back. Damn, if that isn't the hottest thing I've ever seen.

"That was a mistake, red," Dead Man #1 growls, helping Dead Man #4 to his feet. "Now we're going to make your boyfriend watch while we have our fun with you."

I'm going to destroy them for even thinking of touching her. Inara, she's not helpless. I know that, but there are four of them, and they've got weapons. I just need her to get out of here so I can handle this.

"Great punch," I say, my voice steady despite the fire raging inside me. "Now run Inara, get out of here! I'll deal with these losers and I'll be right behind you. We're only a few blocks from my place. Don't stop!"

I strike at Dead Man #1, sweeping his legs out from under him and stealing his weapon before he can react. #3 and #4 come at me together, distracting me—

"Cian!" Inara screams

Dead Man #2 must have finally recovered because I look up to find that he has her in his grip. Ever the fighter, she takes the chance to bite down on his hand and I watch in horror as he smashes her head into the brick wall and lets her body slump to the ground. Everything in me freezes. A cold, visceral dread curls up my spine. He's just killed her. I can feel it in my soul. This isn't just some fight anymore. Everyone is frozen, Abacus is here, ready to collect.

I refuse to accept it. I won't.

I rush to Inara's side, cradling her in my arms, my chest heaving with fury. "I won't let him take you," I whisper, the words a promise.

Abacus steps forward, his cold voice like ice. "I knew my patience would pay off. How sad you spent all that time trying to protect her, only to fail. So where were we, Cian? Oh, yes…the map. Hand it over and I'll let you leave this miserable world with her."

I can feel the weight of his presence, the danger in his voice. But I can't do this alone. Not like this. "Abacus," I say, my voice steady despite the dread crawling up my throat. "I command you to leave. Inara's not ready. Take my life and go."

Nothing happens. It doesn't work. Why isn't it working? Shit, she's out of lives, and my power's useless. What the hell do I do now!

"Cian... it's okay," Inara whispers weakly with tears running down her face, her voice barely a breath. "You have to let me go. Run. Save yourself... save the world." She kisses me, and the weight of her words hits like a freight train. "I love you."

Rage surges through me, something deep and primal.

"I love you too, sweetheart. So, so much. I'm going to fix this," I say as I lay her down gently knowing exactly what I have to do. This ends now. I won't let her die. The thought of her being taken from me is unbearable.

"Cian no" Inara whispers as if sensing I am about to commit something heinous and the truth is—she's right.

Abacus stands there, watching, his endless blue eyes fixated on me like this is all just a game to him and I snap. I don't care what it costs me.

"Enough!" I shout, my voice a roar that shakes the ground beneath me.

I focus, my eyes locking on all four of the mother fuckers who started this. I can see their lives, their beads. The bastard who threw Inara, he only has one bead left. I don't know how I'm doing this but I demand…

"Abacus, you will take his life instead of Inara's. Now, leave." I stand there, unflinching, a breath away from death himself.

The bead burns bright red, and the piece of shit who hurt Inara falls to the ground, dead. Abacus disappears. The others stop in shock, scrambling away, fear in their eyes. Pathetic.

I rush to Inara, pulling her into my arms as she struggles to rise.

"Inara, are you okay?" I ask, my voice shaky despite myself.

"Cian, what did you do?" she breathlessly asks as she stares at his body. Her eyes are filled with concern, but there's something else there too, something I can't quite place. "You took his life for me. Why? Cian, I told you to leave."

I feel a sharp pain in my chest, and my legs give way. I drop to one knee, confusion clouding my thoughts. I don't feel the fear anymore. I should. I should be terrified, but I don't feel anything. What's happening to me? Have I lost another piece of myself?

"Inara..." My voice is hoarse. "I took his life and I would do it again. Abacus would have killed us all. I had no choice." We have to get you somewhere safe." I force the words out, trying to ignore the hollow ache spreading through me.

She's staring at me; her concern more than I can bear. "Cian? Did you hear me? I'm worried about you."

I take her hand, steadying myself. "Sweetheart, I don't know what's happening to me, but we have to keep moving. Let's go home. We can talk more when we're there."

We walk back to my place, hand in hand. I don't know how to fix this, but I know I'll do whatever it takes to keep her safe.

...

I need to regain control before I lose her. When I took that thug's life, I saw fear in her eyes. I understand that fear. Tapping into such raw power unleashed something primal within me, something that even now scratches at the edges of my mind, hungry to return. I lost a piece of myself—my compassion, my restraint—and in its place is this force, this insatiable drive fueled by desire and survival. I'd probably be afraid of it... if I still could feel fear.

We walk the rest of the way home in silence, both pretending we're okay. Even Spencer seems distressed as we make our way down these lifeless streets. The truth hangs between us, unspoken. I killed for her. I'd do it again. And I'm not sure which part of that truth scares her more…the fact that I could, or that I didn't hesitate.

Back inside, I lock the door behind us, double-check the windows, and finally let out a breath I didn't know I was holding. Inara sinks into the couch and rests her head in her hands.

"I need a minute," she says, voice barely above a whisper.

I nod, giving her space, but I can't stop pacing. The weight of what just happened is pressing down on me, but it's dulled now, like I've traded emotion for power. A dangerous exchange. Finally, I sit beside her.

"I didn't want to scare you."

"You didn't." She looks up at me, eyes shimmering with conflict.

"You terrified me."

Ouch. But fair.

"I don't know what's happening to me," I admit.

"But it's like... the more I use the power, the less human I feel. And the worst part is, I liked it."

She shifts closer, her fingers brushing mine.

"You saved my life, Cian. I know you did what you had to do. But I also know you. And this thing, it's not you."

I want to believe her. I really do. But every time I touch that power; it leaves a mark.

"I'm scared of what I'm becoming," I whisper.

"Then let me help you hold onto who you are." She says as she places her hands on either side of my face and forces me to look at her.

I finally meet her gaze, and there's something grounding in her eyes. Steady. Fierce. Loving. She hasn't given up on me. Not yet.

"We'll figure this out," she says, likely more to convince herself than me.

She leans forward, resting her forehead against mine and we both close our eyes and just breath each other in. The gesture bringing me more comfort than she could possibly know. A long silence stretches between us, but it's not uncomfortable. It's full of understanding, of the quiet kind of love that doesn't need grand gestures. Just presence.

Eventually I open my eyes and before I can get too lost in her, I notice her hand, bruised and bleeding. Shame hits me. She punched a guy in the face, and I didn't even notice she was hurt. Way to go, Marine.

"Let me get you some frozen peas and some supplies to clean up your hand."

Inara just sits there, silent and thoughtful, watching as I clean and dress her wound. What I wouldn't give to know what's going on in that beautifully fierce mind of hers. I finish, then gently place a frozen bag of pizza rolls on her hand.

"Sorry. All out of frozen peas." I smile, trying to lighten the mood.

She lets out a soft laugh. "Thank you," she says, kissing my cheek.

I don't deserve her. I should be far away, keeping her safe from all of this, but she's the only thing anchoring me. Without Inara, I fear I'll lose what's left of my humanity. It suddenly hits me that I should write a will, something final, for her.

Everything I have should go to her if I don't make it out of this alive.

"Tomorrow, we can solve this with the others. There must be a reason we were all brought together. We'll come up with a real plan this time. No more improvising," I say shaking off my morose line of thought and getting my head back on mission.

"Next time, we have to stop him because we likely won't get another shot."

Inara nods. "Then let's make this next one count. We should get some rest while we wait for the others to arrive. No telling when I'll have the next opportunity to take advantage of my handsome Marine," she winks and bolts up the stairs giggling.

Fuck, I love her. I'm grinning as I take off after her.

CHAPTER 17
CIAN: HELP WANTED

The crack of thunder jolts me awake. For a moment, I'm disoriented, half-expecting to find myself back in a war zone in the Middle East. Then I remember where I am and almost laugh at the thought, realizing my current reality in Chicago is somehow worse. Inara is still tucked in my arms, her body warm and perfectly molded to mine. Memories of last night rush back, and I know…I've never slept better in my life.

I ease out of bed, careful not to wake her, and head downstairs in search of coffee, letting Inara enjoy some much-deserved rest. At the doorway, I pause for one last look—her fiery hair spilling over the pillow, the steady rise and fall of her breathing. She's breathtaking in my bed, and if we make it through this, I hope it becomes hers too.

…

Footsteps reach my ears and I turn just before Inara launches herself into my arms, yelling, "Trust catch!"
I laugh, catch her effortlessly, and spin us around to settle her gorgeous ass on the counter.

"Morning, handsome," she says, a deviously intoxicating smile curling across her face, pulling me under like a riptide.

Before I can react, her lips are on mine, her hands tangled in my hair, pulling me into her. In that moment, I know, there's nothing I wouldn't destroy for her. I'd set the world on fire and watch it burn, grinning the whole time.

"I'm starving, do we have eggs?" she says, abruptly ending our kiss as quickly as she started it.

I smile loving that she said WE. Before I can respond she fires off another question...

"Actually... do you think the others are going to make it? I'm worried Abacus might go after them because I didn't help him. Do you think Death holds a grudge? I don't think he saw the knife, but what if he did and he goes all Deathier than normal Death?! Is Deathier even a word? And why is email even working when cell phones aren't? Its wild John somehow got our messages don't you think?"

Make that another 5 questions—

"Whoa, slow down, killer. One, they'll make it because we need them to make it. Two, I'm pretty sure John's been preparing for the end of days his whole life." I respond and begin making her some scrambled eggs before she decides to eat me instead.

"Three, email is the best way to communicate during emergencies. The military designed networks that will still function even when all other methods of communication go down. The laptop we've been using from Clare's wild tech stash in the basement seems to function in a similar manner.

Presidential, almost. I've seen one like it before on a black ops mission…we were called off before we could secure it, but I'd never forgot the sleek metal casing."

What were you into, Clare?

"Four, Deathier might just be my new favorite word." I say, setting a plate of food in front of her and kissing her forehead.

"How did you know I love the dramatic effect of a good list?!" Inara quips

"Because I know you sweetheart" I smirk

We sit eating breakfast in a comfortable silence, the kind that feels like it could become my favorite routine. Inara's voice breaks through my thoughts of the future I hope to have with her.

"Cian, come on. We should check the basement again—maybe your mom left something that can help us stop Abacus," she says, releasing my hand as she heads for the door.

"You're right, as always. Who knows? Maybe she left another sword down there," I joke with a laugh.

We descend into the hidden bunker Clare built for me and get to work.

"I'll start with these boxes. Maybe she wrapped up all the answers we need like a gift," I say, pulling out old files and strange artifacts Clare tucked away.

After a while, I stand and stretch, dust clinging to my hands. I exhale deeply and let myself take in the sight of Inara spinning lazily in a chair, her smile lighting the room and warming my chest. For a second, I feel like me again. Hold onto this, Cian. Don't lose it again. But like a raccoon clutching cotton candy in the rain—it vanishes.

This feeling, it's like my first month back from deployment. I was a powder keg, ready to blow over a sideways glance. Picked fights with people who I knew would hit back. It didn't ease up until I met Inara and Vale. That group meeting changed more than I realized. It helped me start healing, and now I'm dragging them all into this. If something happens to them... that's on me.

...

Help is coming. I should feel relieved. Instead, the weight feels heavier. Charlie, Vale, John—they've become my family. I can't lose them. Not to him. Not again. I'll kill Death himself before I let that happen.

Memories flicker—Charlie at Christmas. She was an orphan, bounced through homes until she aged out. I guess that's why birthdays and holidays mean so much to her now. Inara and Vale planned a surprise Christmas party for her a few months ago and made John and me help.

I'm glad they did. The cake alone, Italian buttercream from a bakery Inara found, was worth it. Girl has a gift for sniffing out desserts. We decorated the art gallery, brought presents, and Vale even hauled in a six-foot live tree. The needles were a nightmare, but worth it. Peggy was in Greece, so she didn't protest.

It was one of the best holidays I've ever had. Inara even gave me a gift. The party was supposed to be for Charlie, but she slipped me something too, a five-pound bag of gummy worms and a little Marine bear that sings when you squeeze his paw.

♪ "From the halls of Montezuma... To the shores of Tripoli..." ♪

I still have it in my closet.

Charlie cried when she walked in. We all did, a little. At the next meeting, she surprised everyone with personalized gifts, always thinking of others. She brought treats every week. That's just who she is.

…

"Ding dong" The familiar chime of the doorbell echoes down the stairs.

"That has to be them," Inara says, sprinting upward like she's flying.

I chase after her, closing the gap and reach the door just as she swings it open. A hundred terrible scenarios flicker through me—curious neighbors, a prank, or worse, someone sent to hurt us. Relief slams into my chest when I see familiar faces instead of the shadow of Death.

"Where's Charlie?" Inara asks before the others can get a word out.

Vale trembles like she's made of glass. Tears spill down her cheeks as she tries to form words that won't come out.

"John, what happened?" I demand, holding my hand out for a shake like I'm anchoring myself to normalcy.

He doesn't take it. Instead, he collides into me in a hug so hard it steals my breath. That kind of reaction leaves no room for anything hopeful.

He got her, my brain whispers, and Vale finally forces it out between sobs.

"Charlie's dead."

Inara folds into me like a broken thing. Her whole body goes slack against mine.

"How?" she chokes.

"We don't know," Vale says, wiping her face with the back of her hand. She breathes deep, trying to pull herself together. "John went to grab her and when she didn't answer the door, he used the spare key. I still can't believe it's real. She was…laying on the floor, lifeless."

"Cian, can you bring her back?" John asks, desperation raw in his voice.

My mouth opens, but the truth is a stone. There is a way, yes, the same thing Abacus hunts for. I could bring Charlie back if I had the gem. If I knew where it is. If I knew how to use it. None of those are possible in this moment.

"I'm sorry, John. There's nothing I can do." I keep my voice steady even though everything inside me is ragged.

"We need a drink." I say and rush off to grab the whiskey while I collect my thoughts.

The bottle feels heavier than normal when I hold it up. "Who's in?"

"Good idea," Vale whispers.

"I could use one after today." She looks at Inara; who only nods.

"Can't hurt," John adds in a voice that tries to hide his devastation and fails.

I pour shots, place the bottle on the counter, raise my glass.

"For Charlie." I tap the rim and slam it back. Everyone follows suite.

We drift into the living room to sit, to make space for decisions we can't yet make. A sharp pain knifes through my chest and I go to one knee for a moment and it passes just as quickly.

"Cian, are you ok?" A concerned Inara asks.

As I settle back, my gaze lands on Vale's painting on the wall and my throat closes. The face she painted stares out with a cold, unreadable smile.

"It's him," I blurt.

"Cian, what wrong?" Inara's hand finds mine. Her eyes are all worry.

"Abacus." I say the name like a warning.

I can't shake those empty, predatory eyes, or the smile that doesn't reach them. Vale watches me, steady now.

"You aren't making any sense" Inara says.

"I need to get something; I will be right back." I bolt for the basement, fingers fumbling through dust until I find the old journal.

I run back up, heaving for a breath of air through my panic.

"Here—look." I slam the journal open to a sketch that matches the painting down to the crooked smile. Underneath, a name: Jameson Case.

"Vale, I think this is what Abacus looked like when he was human. He was Jameson."

"Inara, don't you recognize him? He hasn't been shifting forms anymore." I say and reach for her hands to steady her.

"He's right," Vale says, quiet but sure.

"How do you know I am right?" I push.

"Vale paints the deaths she sees, and must have seen him thousands of times since this all started." Inara says.

The room tilts, sudden and small, like a ship correcting course. I don't have time to unpack that at the moment but we will get back to how Vale has been hiding something so massive from all of us, well most of us. We need to find a way to stop the end of the world, and going down the rabbit hole on why Vale can see death taking lives will surely delay that mission.

"I would like another drink, if that's ok?" John interrupts with his awkward request and makes us all pause for moment.

"Me too." Vale says and Inara nods as I start to pour another round.

Silence sits between us for a beat, then shifts into strategy. We go down to the basement to continue researching Jameson Case with hope to unlock his secrets. He once was a human man, maybe we can get through to him and make him stop this.

...

"We've been debating tactics for hours," John says.

"We know this sword can hurt him, maybe even kill him. Problem is I can't get close enough. He teleports, reads minds, steals lives in a blink. Ideas?" I say defeated.

"Maybe we lie to him," Vale says, rubbing her temples.

"Tell him if he puts everything back to normal some magical spell will save him or that we have what he is looking for."

John mutters, "Maybe we should run," as if running were a real option.

Inara shakes her head slowly.

"We can't outrun Death, John." She says and gives him a look like he is in trouble for not doing his homework.

"Cian, what did Clare actually do for a living?" Vale asks.

"This bunker, the gear, the tech—it's insane. CIA? Black ops?" John adds in.

"I thought I knew everything about her, but the truth is... I didn't know Clare at all," I admit, flipping through another file about cave paintings and how the first with the ability to cheat Death was thousands of years ago.

"Hear me out," John says.

"What if we find the gem and fix this ourselves? Yeah, the map's gone, but maybe there's another copy, or we find it on our own. Does that journal mention anything, Cian?" He says and reaches out to see if I would let him read it.

I nod slowly.

"That was my first thought too, but without the map, it'll take too long and I read the journal five times already and there is no other information on its whereabouts." I say and return to reading the file in my hand.

My eyes blur from hours of reading. Angels. Labyrinths. Beast myths. Why did Clare have all this? Was any of it real? Maybe she was losing her mind. Or maybe she knew something I don't, yet. What if this is all connected somehow?

"Cian," Vale says, waving a stack of files.

"What if we just drive around and look for people dying? We might spot Abacus and then you can just shoot him."

I look at the guns lining the bunker wall and understand why she would suggest such a thing to a Marine. It's not the worst idea, but it is up there when you remember he is the immortal death and cannot be killed, at least not with a gun.

"Vale, I like it but I went off on my own to try that and it never goes as planned. We need something that he won't see coming." I answer and look at Inara and find her face scrunched up like when she has a secret.

What is she hiding?

CHAPTER 18
CIAN: LAST STAND

"Cian, what if we try searching the numbers from the map? Maybe they're coordinates, a parcel ID, or a phone number?" Inara smiles as she says it, clearly forgetting that I burned the map to keep it from Abacus and John had just brought up the same idea to no avail.

That smile gets me every time, though. I know the world is in danger and we could die any second, but I can't stop dreaming of a lifetime of those smiles.

"Sweetheart... I burned the map." I say with a grin.

"Amazing idea, though. I bet those numbers would've helped us figure this out." I wrap my arms around her waist and pull her in for a kiss.

"Promise you won't be mad?" she asks, her voice hesitant, and dripping with guilt.

"Why would I be mad?" I ask, curious.

"I, uh... might've taken a picture of the map with my phone before you burned it. I thought it might be important. I didn't tell you because, well, you said Abacus could read minds. I figured it was safer if only I knew." She says and starts to squirm like prey while I process this new information.

I can't stay mad at her, even if I wanted to. Damn, she's brilliant. Her logic's solid, and thanks to her, we have options again. The knot in my stomach eases. For the first time since I took that waiter's life, hope creeps back in. She is always showing me the light.

"Mad? I'm thrilled," I say, sweeping her up into my arms for a much-deserved kiss.

"You just gave us our best shot at stopping Abacus and saving the world. I love you. Admittedly, burning the map so soon may not have been my best idea."

"Okay, you two, that's enough. Show us this map," John chimes in, clearly impatient.

I take in John for a moment realizing it is likely hard for him to watch us when he's still grieving Charlie, and what he never got the chance to say. There are few things as devastating as words left unspoken. I set Inara down, and she hands me her phone, the image of the map appears on the screen.

"I wish they were coordinates, but this looks like ten consecutive numbers. Maybe it's a phone number," I say, passing the phone to John and Vale to examine.

"Cell towers are still down, so we can't try calling it," Vale points out.

"Cian, can we use your supercomputer?" John asks eager to get his hands on it.

I nod, and he dives into Clare's computer, punching in the numbers and hitting enter. A beat passes. Then the results pop up. Out of five million hits, one stands out…a phone number to a bank here in Chicago.

"No way," John says. "The gem is in a bank!"

"That's Clare's bank," I mutter, stunned.

"I took over her account there, but I never use it."

"Well, what are we waiting for? Let's go get the gem!" John says, already on his feet.

"All the banks are shut down because, y'know, the apocalypse," Inara says, gently reminding him.

"Are we really about to Mission: Impossible this place? We don't even know if the gems actually there. It could just be a clue to start that journey," Vale says in a panicked rush.

"If we find the gem, Abacus will just take it from us anyway. This can't be our only plan." I say, already loading gear into a duffel as a plan begins to form.

"We don't know how to use it yet. The main mission hasn't changed: we find Abacus, distract him, and I kill him."

"Okay… then what?" John asks.

"We improvise. I'm going to offer Abacus a counterfeit gem, then strike when he lets his guard down to retrieve it," I say, watching Inara's face fall into worry.

No risk, no reward. This is a Hail Mary, but time's up and I believe it can work. This has to work.

"That's not a plan," Vale says.

"You really think Abacus will drop his guard over a gem? What if he reads your mind and knows it's fake? And do we even know where to find him?"

"This'll work," I say, confidence surging.

"It's not my first rodeo. I'll go alone. Tell him I have what he wants, and that I can end his suffering. If he reads my mind, he'll see the truth, because this sword will end him. One way or another and I have been practicing on my mental barriers. While I'm doing this, you guys go to the bank to figure out what Clare left for me using any means necessary."

"As for finding him?" I shrug.

"I can jump off a bridge or step in front of a moving car. That usually does the trick in an instant."

"I hate this plan!" Inara snaps.

"You could really die this time. Why can't we do this together?"

She looks to Vale and John for support, but they stay silent, their fear obvious. I can't blame them. Facing Abacus where they can't move, is suicide. Taking them with me would only give him leverage and lead to more death.

"We're out of time. He'll find us any minute. I have to go to him first and end this. It has to be me, love. And it will give you time to find whatever is at that bank."

I reach for her, but she pulls away, walking to the other end of the room. The house suddenly feels enormous, like she's an entire world away. She's afraid I won't come back. She's right to be. This mission has a low chance of success and a high chance of death, like the others. I want to lie and promise I'll return, but fate is not likely on my side this time.

"Inara, I can't lose you, or anyone else I care about. The fake gem gives me the element of surprise. He won't expect me to attack if he thinks he's already won." I turn to Vale.

"You're crafty. Want to help me counterfeit a huge green gem? I think Clare had some jewels in that trunk behind you."

…

Inara finds us in the kitchen, putting the final touches on the fake gem. Without a word, she walks up, grabs my face, and kisses me hard…God, I love this woman.

If I don't stop Abacus, everything ends. But right now, she's all I want. I pull her close, letting myself feel everything, her body, her warmth, her love. This might be the last time I ever get to touch her. I'm about to kill myself for a one-on-one with Death, lie to someone who can read minds, and fight with nothing but a sword. I must be insane.

"Hey, you two. Get a room," Vale teases from across the kitchen.

I don't care. The whole world could be watching, and I still wouldn't stop. I want to remember every inch of her before I go. But then... I feel it. That gut-deep sense of dread, cold and crawling. My body knows what my mind won't admit. Abacus is coming. And I have to go.

"Hey guys, the sky looks pretty bad out there, and it's raining again. I don't think we have much longer," John says, right before a massive lightning strike hits nearby and knocks the power out again.

"The gem looks great, Vale! Just give me a sec, and then I'll go jump off a bridge," I say, trying to lighten the mood, but it falls flat.

Everyone's clouded in sadness, weighed down by the uncertainty of our fates. I can do this.

"You better come back, Cian," Vale says and punches me in the arm.

"Do you really think you can stop Abacus?" John asks, arms open for a hug.

"Yes," I say with a wink, then push Vale into his arms to take the hug for me.

"Cian, what the—" Vale starts, but then she just leans into it. She needed a hug after all.

"John, Vale, good luck at the bank. See why Clare left that phone number on the map. Here's my account info and a key I found in the basement. Might be for a deposit box. If I fail, it's on you to find the real gem and stop Abacus. Feel free to check the basement for any clues or gear. But don't stay too long, if I die, he may come here looking for it," I say, trying to show them I care without actually saying it.

"Of course. We won't let you down," John replies and hugs me anyway.

"Cian, I love you. You got this, man" Vale says, letting a few tears fall, knowing this might be goodbye.

I have no idea how this will go, but having them as a backup plan gives me some peace. I should probably tell them not to use the gem to bring me back, but the thought is oddly comforting, so I keep that to myself and go find Inara. She's in the basement, stockpiling weapons like she's heading into war. Which is insane.

"What are you doing?" I ask, casually.

"Packing more supplies. For us," she says, like it's no big deal.

Wait…she thinks she's coming with me. No way. She's on her last life. If Abacus gets to her, he'll use her to destroy me.

"I've already got what I need. You're taking Spencer and my car and getting as far away from here as possible," I say, handing her the keys.

She freezes, still holding a knife in her left hand, and looks up at me with those emerald eyes. And just like that, I forget what I was going to say. Those eyes always get me in trouble. I laugh quietly at myself and smile. This is likely goodbye, and it's tearing me apart, but there's no other way. I'm the only one who can do this. Still… I'm afraid saying no will get me stabbed.

"Did you really think I'd leave the fate of the world to you alone? That's cute," she says with a smirk.

"This is bigger than us and you're sweet, but I'm exhausted with the chivalry routine. You need me out there if this plan's going to work. We only get one shot."

I should keep pushing her to leave but I cave. I agree. I tell myself she's safer with me anyway, because I'll die before I let anything happen to her. Abacus could strike anywhere, so what's the difference if she's next to me when it all goes down?

"As you wish. You ready, sweetheart?" I ask, gesturing to the stairs.

"After you. And I can carry my own bag," she says, swatting my hand away as I reach for the green rucksack overflowing with weapons.

Before we leave, we get Spencer geared up in his harness for his bank heist with Aunty Vale. She takes his leash, we hug it out, possibly for the last time and we go our separate ways.

"Want to drive?" I ask as Inara and I head out to the car.

"Of course!" she says, jumping into the driver's seat just as I open her door like a gentleman.

So many thoughts race through my mind as I stare out the window at a city I no longer recognize. The storms could be beautiful if they weren't signaling the end of everything. Purple streaks flash through the sky, like fireworks on the Fourth of July.

...

"I love you, sweetheart. If I fail, promise me you won't use the gem to bring me back," I say, holding her hands.

"This has to work," she says, intentionally dodging the promise.

"Promise me," I repeat, more firmly.

"Okay. I promise. But you're going to beat him and come back to me," she says, kissing me.

"Thank you. Now please... wait in the car," I say before walking to the edge of the bridge.

Diving from this height should kill me. And with the storm raging, the water below looks more like an ocean. Worst case, I drown. I glance back at Inara one last time, trying to burn every detail into my memory.

"Inara, no! Stop!" I yell, jumping back to the pavement and sprinting toward her, but I'm too late.

She steps in front of a speeding car. Everything freezes. Abacus is here. I rush to her and draw my sword. He's nowhere in sight but the sword glows. I've got the fake gem ready in my pocket.

"I couldn't let you do it. I love you, Cian. Now go stop Abacus. Don't worry about me," she says as I help her to her feet.

I'm furious, but damn, I'm also in awe. Her bravery never stops surprising me.

"Baby, you shouldn't have done that, but I promise, I won't waste this chance," I say, still scanning for Abacus.

Then he appears, right behind us—and suddenly I'm flying through the air into the railing. The sword flies from my hand. He's never gotten this physical before. I must be getting under his skin.

"Abacus, there's no need for that," I say, trying to mask my thoughts.

"We called you here to end this. I have what you need. I'll help you end the curse."

He locks eyes with me, then turns to Inara and without hesitation, snaps her neck. He doesn't even remove her bead from the abacus. I didn't know you could die in the in-between realm. My body goes numb.

"No!" I scream—a raw, soul-shaking cry—as I watch the love of my life fall.

I dive for the sewer grate, grab the sword, and leap to my feet but he's just watching me. Amused. The pain morphs into something sharper, hotter. The sword feels like justice in my hand.

"You're going to die for taking her!" I roar, charging. But he vanishes before I get halfway there.

"Bring her back!" I shout.

He's taken his last life. I won't fail again. Fueled by rage and a supernatural surge, I swing with all my might and I hit something. He cries out in pain. I strike again. And again. The sword glows brighter with each blow. But he still stands.

"How?" I gasp, watching as he heals before I can recover from my last attack.

He raises his fist, but I'm faster. I slide the sword straight into his chest.

"Fool. I have no heart," Abacus sneers, then vanishes.

I'm not getting anywhere with body blows. Think, Cian. The abacus ring…it has to be the source of his power. I pull the gem from my pocket and hold it up, hoping he'll take the bait.

"Is that the gem?" Abacus says from behind me. In a blink, he's standing in front of me, reaching for it.

I bring the blade down, severing his hand and with it, his grip on the abacus. He locks eyes with me, a strange familiarity flashing across his face, and he smiles.

"There you are, my dear," he says, and then turns to dust.

"I actually did it. I stopped him, Inara," I whisper, forgetting for a moment that she's gone.

The sword clatters to the ground, its blue glow fading. I did it. I killed him. But I'm all alone. I look to her lifeless body... and turn away. Then I see it, the golden shimmer of the abacus ring. Just lying there. Maybe... maybe I can still use it to save her. I just need to give her one of my lives. As I step closer, a wave of energy floods through me. It's like the abacus knows—knows I'm willing to give everything I have to bring her back.

"Please bring her back. I'll do whatever it takes," I say to the inanimate object as I pick up the golden ring.

It's surprisingly lightweight and feels good in my hand. The abacus begins to glow brightly, and I know my plan is working. Two rows of beads appear—one for Inara, and the other must be mine. I've never seen it up close before. It's beautiful. The beads are gemstones, black as night, and the way the light dances inside them makes it feel like they contain a piece of our souls. Something guides me as I pull back a handful of Inara's beads, not stopping until they lock into place on the other side. The beads glow green for a moment, and then I see Inara's body begin to move. I barely get to say her name before I'm swallowed whole by the nothingness.

The rows that were there a moment ago are gone—even the one I believed was mine. I've never seen it empty before. It kind of reminds me of a wedding band, just much larger. Where am I? This place is bizarre, to put it mildly. I traded my life for Inara's, and now I'm dead? This isn't what I pictured as the next realm. It's more like limbo but without buildings, without anything. There's nothing here. Just endless darkness. I try to open my hand to drop the ring, now that I'm done with it, but that's harder than expected. It's stuck to my palm and won't let go. I wave my hand like it's on fire and even try throwing it like a football, but no luck. The abacus is now stuck to me.

I feel something changing inside me, just like the other night when my eyes turned blue. Only this time, it doesn't hurt. I can't feel anything at all. A loud, shrill sound screeches behind me and snaps my attention toward it. I look around the vast empty space and catch movement in the distance. What the hell makes a noise like that? My brain races to come up with something that makes even a little sense. A moose? A ghost? I laugh at myself.

My mind lands on a dragon, but only because that would be the coolest thing to happen out of all this. Shame they don't exist. The sound comes again, louder, closer. The abacus starts to vibrate in my hand, its light growing in intensity. Then—I see them. The creatures, impossibly large and wrapped in shadows.

They're closing in fast. I brace for a fight. All I can think about is Inara, lying in the street. I saw her open her eyes…she has to be okay. But there's a pull in my chest, a warning, like my body knows something I don't. A piercing cry rips through my ears as the massive creature drops in front of me and lunges. I reach for my sword only to remember I dropped it after killing Abacus. Hopefully, it's still with Inara.

My gaze drops to my hand. The golden ring blazes bright green—then begins to change.

"What are you doing?" I ask the glow, as if it can answer.

The abacus twists, reshaping into something I know instantly. When the light dies, I'm holding a sword. Its solid gold with intricate designs etched along the blade. The hilt holds a lifeline, though all its beads are gone. The edge gleams wickedly as I raise it, ready to meet the oncoming attack. The creature is still enveloped in darkness, its form shifting, but I'm set.

"Come on!" I roar as it closes in.

But before my blade can meet it, the thing is ripped apart from above. What the hell? This has to be a dream. Did Abacus win? Am I trapped here as his plaything? Because there's no way I'm actually seeing this.

"It's alright, Cian. I'll explain what's happening to you. But first, I'm not making the same mistake I did with your predecessor. You'll be allowed to retain your memories, as long as you follow my commands," says an angelic being as it floats down from above.

Is this an angel—am I—

"Don't fret. You're safe while I'm here in the Void. Also, I can read your mind. And no, this is not a dream. I accepted your offer," the being says, hovering closer.

So many questions flood my mind, but all I can do is stare at the wings. It has to be. I'm in the presence of—

"All things will come in time. We need to make this official."

The being's tone sharpens.

"Cian, do you swear to maintain the natural order of all life in the universe, and to account for every living soul, forever?"

"What?" I ask, confused and still trying to understand what's happening to me.

Am I supposed to be... the new Abacus? I remember now, I did promise to do anything to save her.

"Ding! Ding! You got it. Now you're showing some promise. For a moment, I thought I'd need to find someone else. This is a sacred responsibility. Once accepted, it cannot be undone. You'll serve a purpose far greater than your feeble mortal mind could've ever comprehended."

"Now, hold up the angelic instrument and swear your obedience to the natural order. Swear to serve us. Forever."

"I think there's some confusion here. I already served my time in the Marines, and this natural order thing... doesn't really sound like a good fit. Can you just drop me back off in Chicago? I ha—"

"Think of me like your drill instructor at basic, Cian. This is not up for debate. You don't want to test an angel."

"...Yes, sir."

It hurts to say it. I want to fight back. I want to go back to her. But he said angel and drill instructor in the same sentence and I immediately feel the urge to jump into position of attention.

"Good."

He pats my head like I'm a child.

"I am the archangel, Gabriel. From now on, you are my servant. Your duty is to account for all life and death, and to maintain the order Fate demands. Disobey us and, well—I think you get it."

I don't know what to do. Do I just... start cleaning up Jameson's mess? What does that even look like? Gabriel is intense and staring a hole through me.

"You may begin by cleansing this Void of the tormented souls your failed predecessor discarded after stealing their lifelines. I see you've already bonded with it. It'll make short work of these deformed souls."

"You're telling me... these creatures used to be human?" I ask, stunned.

"A soul should never be left in purgatory. This is what happens when they are neglected. When you're finished here, you'll begin restoring order on Earth and so on until you have restored balance. And you will never speak to a human or attempt to interact with them again. Violate that, and your punishment will be immediate."

I glance down at the glowing abacus that is now a sword in my hand. The weight of it feels heavier than ever. In the past year, I've seen more than I thought possible—Abacus nearly tearing the universe apart, his mind unraveling piece by piece. He had to be stopped. But his last moment still burns in my memory—the way his eyes shifted after I struck the final blow. Not rage. Not hatred. Regret. He was just a man who carried

Death's burden for too long and it broke him. Will I end the same way?

The thought coils through me like smoke, impossible to shake.

"I am Death now." I whisper resolute in my fate.

And now, I must serve for the greater good, and to spare the woman I love for as long as it takes. Forever.

I scan the endless expanse around me, searching for a way to help them all. Then my gaze snags on a face in the crowd, one I know all too well, and never hoped to see here.

"Charlie? Is that you?" I take a slow step toward the lost spirit.

"Charlie! I reach for her shoulders, but my hands pass straight through.

Right. She's a ghost now—no body to hold, and I'm Death. If anyone can snap her out of this trance, it has to be me.

"Charlie, it's Cian. Look at me!" Power thrums in my voice, lightning surging through my veins.

"Cian?" she whispers, her eyes beginning to lift toward mine.

"Where am I?" The question trembles out of her as her memories begin to flood back.

"Abacus took all your lives. You've been trapped here in the void ever since. But I'm here now, and I'm going to fix this." I glance over my shoulder at the angel, searching for answers.

"You have no choice now. She must be taken to her next realm," Gabriel says and vanishes as abruptly and ominously as he appeared.

Fuck. I can't save her. What good is being Death if I can't? And what happens if Inara loses a life? Will I be the one forced to take her?

A burn ignites in my chest, sharp and relentless and then fades into a cold, hollow numbness. I don't know why, but suddenly, I don't care who lives or dies. Am I losing myself already? No. Not yet. Not until I've saved Charlie from this place. I close my eyes. When I open them, my hand is already extending the abacus toward her, my body moving like it's done this a thousand times.

"Cian, I'm scared," she says, tears slipping down her ghostly face.

"It's going to be alright. Trust me." I lie, because I have no idea what I'm doing or if it will be okay.

Her fingers brush the beads. A blinding, white-hot light erupts, swallowing her whole. For a heartbeat, I glimpse a gate made of pure energy and feel the same watching presence I felt when Gabriel appeared. Heaven. It has to be. Then she's gone. And I'm alone in the void, surrounded by thousands of lost souls waiting to be ferried to their rest. There's a strange beauty in it. It's time to embrace my destiny as Death or risk becoming as mad as the one who came before me.

"I'm sorry, Inara," I whisper, before beginning my endless mission to restore the balance between life and death for the universe.

End of Book One

Thank you for reading. Book Two is coming soon and will begin with Inara waking—only to find herself alone.

Made in the USA
Coppell, TX
27 February 2026

72454249R00177